This Last Adventure

Ryan Dalton

🌿 CAROLRHODA BOOKS

MINNEAPOLIS

Carolrhoda Books®
An imprint of Lerner Publishing Group, Inc.
241 First Avenue North
Minneapolis, MN 55401 USA

For reading levels and more information, look up this title at www.lernerbooks.com.

Cover illustration by Chiara Fedele.

Main body text set in Bembo Std.
Typeface provided by Monotype Typography.

Library of Congress Cataloging-in-Publication Data

Names: Dalton, Ryan (Young adult author) author.
Title: This last adventure / Ryan Dalton.
Description: Minneapolis : Carolrhoda Books, 2022. | Audience: Ages 10–14. |
    Audience: Grades 4–6. | Summary: "When Archie's beloved grandpa is diagnosed
    with Alzheimer's disease, Archie tries to slow the progression of his grandpa's
    memory loss through shared role-playing fantasies. But he has to face the reality of
    what he's losing." —Provided by publisher.
Identifiers: LCCN 2021004145 | ISBN 9781541599284
Subjects: CYAC: Grandfathers—Fiction. | Alzheimer's disease—Fiction. |
    Imagination—Fiction.
Classification: LCC PZ7.1.D29 Th 2022 | DDC [Fic]—dc23

LC record available at https://lccn.loc.gov/2021004145

Manufactured in the United States of America
1-48202-48774-8/6/2021

To Austin

FOR ALL THE REASONS YOU FORGOT
FROM THOSE WHO REMEMBER

Chapter 1

Grandpa didn't recognize me today.

Archie Reese tried to say the words, but they wouldn't come out.

He poked at his breakfast while Mom bustled around the kitchen. He tried thinking about his eggs and toast, or the way Mom talked to herself while she made his lunch. The academy served great lunches, but they were expensive. For him, anyway.

Thinking about food didn't work, so he tried focusing on the school day ahead. But his brain kept returning to what had happened thirty minutes ago, and to similar incidents from the past few months. Moments Archie had dismissed at the time because they had only seemed like random incidents.

This morning had been different. This morning had felt like what his seventh-grade health teacher described in class last year. There had been a week when they talked about—

"Alley-oop!"

A slice of cheese flew across the kitchen. With an audible slap, it landed next to an open ham sandwich. Mom pumped her fist.

"Yes! Two points."

Despite his mood, Archie laughed. "You missed."

"But I got close. That's worth partial credit."

"Oh, right," Archie said. "I forgot about the almost points they give you in basketball."

"Don't tell me you've actually watched a game," Mom teased. "The world may crumble."

"I've read Kwame Alexander's books. That's close enough."

Mom chuckled. She was in a good mood today. No, more than just good. She was acting silly, which meant she was extra happy. Archie always noticed when that happened; for one thing, it tended to be a good time to ask for favors.

He wondered where it was coming from today. She liked her job as a dental hygienist, but she went every day, so that probably wasn't the reason. Maybe she had a date tonight and had forgotten to tell him.

Archie tried to channel some of Mom's positive

energy. Today would be a good day, even if it had started . . . oddly. He reached toward a stack of books on the table and carefully extricated a sci-fi novel from the middle; he'd been wanting to read it for weeks but had forgotten which stack it was in.

He and Grandpa kept books all over the house. Last year, they'd spent months one-upping each other by finding increasingly random places to hide books within easy reach. Archie had thought he'd won by hiding a copy of *White Fang* in the freezer between two steaks. Then Grandpa had taken the prize by wrapping *The Sea Wolf* in plastic and taping it under the toilet tank lid.

The memory made Archie smile. Until it crashed against the memory of this morning and shattered.

You have to say it.

Shoving the thought away, he opened the book and leapt into the first chapter, where a lone ship was marooned in deep space. The story gripped him just like he'd hoped it would, until—

"Do you think you'll have time to split some wood after school?" Mom asked. "I'd like to get the wood-pile built up a little more before it starts getting cold."

His concentration crumbled. He stifled a sigh. "Oh, um, sure."

"Great. Oh, and I was thinking that when Grandpa's with his crew on Wednesday night, you could come by the office after school and then we could pick up dinner on the way home."

"Yeah, cool. As long as Zahira won't mind me doing homework in the waiting room."

"Are you kidding? You'll be someone new to talk to. She'll probably pull up a chair for you at the reception desk."

Mom turned away, and he dove into the book again. But this time the world on the page didn't come to life for him, and the characters didn't act out the scene in his mind like a movie. His bubble of fantasy kept bursting as the memory grew more insistent, refusing to be put aside.

Archie and Grandpa had their morning routine. The same conversation, to get the day started right. Until now, Archie never realized how much he needed it.

"Morning, Grandpa," he would say.

"Morning, Fletch. Ready for battle?" Grandpa would respond every time. Fletch was his nickname for Archie, though he would never explain why.

"Always," Archie would reply.

"Good! Then suit up."

That was how it should have happened. That was how it always happened.

Until today.

Instead . . .

~~~

Half an hour earlier, Archie had mumbled his usual groggy "Morning," as he passed Grandpa's door.

As usual, the door was open. Raymond Reese got up at impossibly early hours and had long since started his day, while Archie still shambled around like a zombie. He slowed his steps, waiting for Grandpa's reply.

Except the reply didn't come. Archie paused in his grandfather's doorway.

Raymond Reese sat in his recliner, scanning the newspaper. He wore neatly pressed slacks and a button-up shirt with freshly polished shoes. Even for someone as put together as Grandpa, that was unusual.

"Um . . . Grandpa?"

Grandpa looked up, lowering the newspaper, and gave Archie a friendly smile. But it was the smile he gave to strangers.

"Morning, sir," Grandpa said. "Are you the manager? I'd like to check out today, so you can send them to clean the room. That work for you?"

It wasn't a joke. Grandpa's eyes always twinkled when he joked. This was real to him.

For a long moment, Archie could only stare at his grandfather, feeling completely lost. Should he explain who he was, and where they were, until the light returned to Grandpa's eyes?

"Um . . ." Archie began.

Then he turned and fled. Hiding in the bathroom, he took a long, scalding shower and tried to put the exchange out of his mind. Maybe he'd dreamed it. Sometimes dreams didn't fade when you woke up.

He felt a little better after that. But then, as he was walking back to his room—

"Morning, Fletch. Ready for battle?"

Archie stopped short. Slowly he turned to look into Grandpa's room.

The gaze that met his was no longer empty. Somehow his grandfather was Raymond Reese again. It was clear on his face—he knew who Archie was and where they were.

He didn't remember that they'd already spoken.

~~~

Archie's insides were cold. He couldn't deny the memory any longer. Couldn't ignore the symptoms the teacher had talked about in health class. Felicity Gordon had even talked about her grandmother having it.

The disease that attacked your mind and stole your memories. Then it stole your personality, your talents and skills, and your ability to function in the world, until there was nothing left but a shell that looked like you.

"Mom," Archie tried to say, but it stuck in his throat.

"Touchdown," Mom said, laughing to herself as she tossed chips into his sandwich bag.

Other memories hit Archie from all sides—ones that hadn't seemed important until now. Just random moments by themselves. His whole family had pretended they didn't mean anything.

Grandpa misplacing his phone, then finding it inside the shoe he was wearing. Forgetting where they lived and driving to the fire station, where he'd worked for so many years before retiring. Forgetting Grandma's name until he looked at old pictures of them together.

Mom did need to know. Archie felt that urgently now, as all the little moments clicked together into one big picture.

"Mom," he said.

"Dad, your eggs are getting cold!" she called, not hearing him. "Are you coming down?"

Archie pushed past the fear and put as much power into his voice as he could.

"MOM!"

She flinched in surprise. "Yeah?"

He couldn't stop now. Holding his mother's gaze, Archie took a deep breath and made himself say it.

Chapter 2

Adults never talked about their time in middle school. Archie hadn't realized that until he started eighth grade six weeks ago. That was when they started saying, "One more year until high school. You're going to love it." Then they'd tell him as many old high school stories as he could sit through.

The only exception was Grandpa, who seemed to have stories for every period of Archie's life. Over the years, Archie had come to anticipate them.

If Archie asked him today about eighth grade, though, would he be able to tell his stories? And even if he could tell them today, would he be able to next week, or next year?

"Dude," someone said over his right shoulder. "Your character just died."

Blinking, Archie looked up. "Huh?"

Zigfried Kahananui, his best friend, sat down next to him at their usual cafeteria table. He nodded at the phone in Archie's hands. "You can't frag aliens by staring at the screen, bro. Not until they make *way* better VR."

Oh, right, the game. He'd been distracting himself with it until his mind drifted again.

He'd been doing that a lot the past few weeks, ever since that morning with Grandpa. He'd scraped together enough courage to tell Mom, and then her eyes had looked like dark clouds. She'd spent the rest of the day researching doctors and making appointments.

"Yeah, um, this level's really tough," Archie said.

"Want a hand? I cleared it last week."

"Nah, I'll figure it out. Thanks, though."

Archie's eyes drifted to the lunch bag that Zig had just set on the table. The scents drifting from the open top were mouthwatering—citrus and spices and some kind of seafood.

With a flourish, Zig pulled out two small containers and handed one over. "Free sample," he said. "You'll love this one."

"Awesome, thanks." Archie dove in. Like always, Zig's lunch was amazing. Archie had enough food at home, but cooking wasn't exactly his family's specialty.

Zig always brought his lunch, even though Blue Sun Academy served practically gourmet food. His family was constantly experimenting with new dishes, and the results often found their way into Zig's bag. His Japanese mom and Hawaiian dad were building a national chain of fusion cuisine restaurants. Their biggest expansion would cover the Midwest, which was why they had moved south of St. Louis a few years ago.

As Archie took a bite of the biggest shrimp he'd ever seen, Zig leaned closer and lowered his voice. "So today's the big day, huh?"

Archie's chewing slowed, an invisible weight settling on his chest. He glanced over at his friend. In place of Zig's usual smile, there was a look of concern.

Swallowing, Archie nodded. "Mom's picking me up after school, then we're going into the city."

"Hang in there, bro," Zig said. "Maybe it'll be good news."

Archie forced a nod. "Thanks, man." After several doctor's appointments, Grandpa expected a final diagnosis today, which meant tension was high for the whole family.

So Archie had been devouring adventure books and role-playing games even faster than usual. Fantasy worlds—even ones with giant monsters—were better than his own right now. At least he could battle monsters head-on.

Soothing flute music floated across the cafeteria—Blue Sun Academy's version of a bell, meaning class would start in a few minutes. Archie still wasn't used to it, but fancy private schools could do that kind of stuff. The headmaster thought bells were too martial.

The music drew clusters of eighth graders out into the halls. After stopping by his locker, Archie joined Zig in US history class.

Blue Sun capped each class at fifteen students to make sure everyone got personal attention, but Archie always felt as if he'd stumbled on a mini-parade celebrating designer clothes and hundred-dollar haircuts. Some of his classmates were already talking about winter break plans in Europe, and it was barely October.

Despite his dark mood, though, Archie felt a flicker of amusement. Listening to these kids was like watching a nature documentary about a different species. It actually made him grateful that he wasn't rich and was only here because Grandpa had set up an education trust when Mom got pregnant. Rich kids were weird. Well, except for Zig.

And except for *her*.

Four girls entered the classroom on a wave of laughter. In the lead was Desta Senai. Her smile lit up the room like a spotlight. Her dark eyes were somehow open and friendly and smoky and mysterious all at once. She wore a blue dress today and had matching pins in her hair.

Speaking of her hair, it was different again. She had started the year with it in twists, then worn it natural for several weeks. Now she'd straightened it into long, flowing locks. And her skin was flawless!

No doubt about it—Desta Senai was stunning. But there were lots of pretty girls in the world. What she did next was the reason Archie could never take his eyes off her.

It always took Desta longer to get to her seat because she greeted every classmate by name along the way. Not sarcastically, either, but like she was actually happy to see them. That smile never wavered—not even when it was Archie's turn.

Yet somehow she always caught him by surprise. He tried to come up with a good response this time, but words escaped him like usual. He settled for just smiling and hoped it wasn't too awkward.

When she reached her seat, Desta pulled her laptop from her bag and immediately started typing up a storm. Probably making notes about one of the dozen school clubs she was in charge of. Archie couldn't guess how she managed it all.

"You're staring," Zig whispered, bumping his elbow.

Archie's neck practically snapped as he turned away as quickly as possible. He shot his friend a grateful look. Zig always watched out for him.

"You might want to think about actually talking to her at some point."

"I'd have to come up with something interesting to say first."

"Phsh. You just need to break the ice." Zig glanced at Desta, then back at Archie, and flashed a mischievous grin. He pulled out his phone.

"Zig, no!" Archie whisper-shouted. "Don't do this to me!"

"Hey, everyone," Zig announced, standing up. "Time for a classie! Gather round."

A classie—that's what Zig called a selfie for a whole class. Ever since he'd named it, dozens of classies had started popping up on social media. Everyone loved Zig, so his idea had immediately turned into a schoolwide trend.

Stifling a groan, Archie stood while Zig worked his magic, rearranging people for the best shot, convincing Spencer Harrington to kneel down in the front since he didn't want to be stuck in the back with the other tall kids, getting everyone to laugh. No one suspected Zig of having a secret plan.

Even Archie didn't realize what was happening until the rearrangements placed Desta right next to him. *Act natural*, he kept telling himself, though he'd somehow forgotten how humans were supposed to hold their arms.

"Okayperfectsmileeveryone!" Zig snapped a dozen pics before Archie could even react.

As the students scattered, Archie remembered it would probably be a good idea if he breathed again soon. Drawing in some air, he turned toward his desk.

And came face-to-face with Desta.

"Cool shirt," she said with a smile that knocked him into next week.

Archie glanced down. He'd worn the Green Arrow shirt today. She liked Green Arrow too? What were the odds?

A bit too late, Archie remembered that humans thanked other humans when they were paid a compliment. "Oh, um, thanks!" he stammered.

Then the moment was over. As everyone sat back down, Zig shot him a covert wink. If he said anything, Archie didn't hear it over the heartbeat pounding in his ears.

Still, as Mr. Gertner started teaching, the anxiety faded and left clarity in its place. She had talked to him—more than just a greeting. And he'd found out they had something in common. He let himself savor the thought.

His phone vibrated. Glancing at his lap, Archie saw a new text from Zig.

—*I hope your granddad's okay. Text me later if you need to.*

Once more, Archie nodded thanks to his best friend.

~~~

Archie bounced in his plush leather chair. This doctor's office was so nice that he could almost forget why they were there.

Almost.

The neurologist had only made a brief appearance in the waiting room, but her white coat had stood out starkly against the soothing earth tones of the office. A reminder of what this place really was.

"Sure is taking a while," Grandpa said from the next chair. He rolled his shoulders in discomfort, stretching his stocky frame. "How many forms will they make Penelope fill out?"

Archie glanced at the front desk, where his mom was scribbling on yet another sheet of paper.

"Maybe it's a kind of test, to find out if you want to see a doctor badly enough," Archie said. He changed his voice to a slow monotone. "Orders signed in triplicate, sent in, sent back, queried, lost, found . . ."

Grandpa nodded, smiling wide. "*The Hitchhiker's Guide to the Galaxy*, Douglas Adams."

"Nailed it," Archie said.

Relaxing back in his chair, Grandpa furrowed his eyebrows. Archie knew what was coming and tried to get his mind ready. They had played this game many times.

"It pays to be obvious, especially if you have a reputation for subtlety," Grandpa quoted.

"Foundation series, Isaac Asimov," Archie replied. "Beware; for I am fearless, and therefore powerful."

"*Frankenstein*, Mary Shelley. How did I escape? With difficulty. How did I plan this moment? With pleasure."

"*The Count of Monte Cristo*, Alexandre Dumas. Is that you, Bong? Or is it James Bong?"

"*Stand Up, Yumi Chung!* Jessica Kim." Grandpa grew sober. As he spoke, the slight midwestern drawl returned to his voice, like it always did when he got serious. "I shouldn't complain. They're going out of their way for me. Just look at 'em go."

He inclined his chin toward the reception area. Two office workers were helping Mom with the paperwork.

Archie nodded in agreement. "Yeah, they probably found out about your background." As soon as he said it, Archie wondered if he should've kept quiet. As a war veteran and a retired firefighter, Grandpa got a lot of automatic respect from strangers, but special treatment made him uncomfortable. Archie decided to change the subject. "So how was it last night?"

At least once a week, Grandpa took dinner to the firehouse and spent the evening with his old friends, many of whom he had trained before retiring.

"Real good. They loved the pork steaks."

"Did you tell them about . . . ?"

"About this? No. They don't need to worry about all that."

Now it was Grandpa's turn to change the subject. He gestured at the book in Archie's lap. "School assignment, or one of yours?"

"Mine," Archie said. "Pretty good so far."

"Got your schoolwork done, first, though. Right?"

Archie grinned. "Of course."

"Well done," Grandpa said. "You haven't talked much about school this year. How's it going?"

"Going great," Archie said. Private school had been a gift from Grandpa, so even on tough days he made sure to be positive. "Classes are good. Zig and I have a few together. Oh, right!"

He remembered now. Zig had sent out the classies from earlier, but Archie had been too preoccupied to look at them. He pulled out his phone and found the message. Enlarging one of the photos, he turned the screen toward Grandpa.

"History class. Mr. Gertner's a total geek like Zig and me, and the rest of the kids are fun."

Well, mostly. No need to tell Grandpa about Spencer Harrington, Blue Sun Academy's best athlete and biggest showboat, and a legend in his own mind. Instead, when he looked at the picture, Archie chose to see the genuine smiles and the—

"So, which one is your crush?"

Archie's head whipped toward his grandfather. "What?"

"Seen that look in young folks' eyes before. I know what it means." Grandpa tapped the screen. "Which one?"

This was the Raymond Reese that Archie had known his whole life. Sharp-witted and observant, with a memory like a vault. He never missed anything.

Maybe what happened before really was a random fluke.

Stifling his embarrassment, Archie pointed. "Her name's Desta."

Grandpa leaned closer to the screen. "Short dark hair and glasses?"

"No, that's Kamiko Sato. Desta's right here, next to me."

Grandpa studied the photo and nodded. "Good smile. Looks genuine. You can tell a lot about someone by their smile. She like you too?"

"Ha. She barely knows who I am. I think we've said about eight words to each other."

"Why? She won't talk to you?"

"No, it's not that. I've never worked up the nerve to start an actual conversation with her."

"How come?"

"It's just . . ."

Archie chewed his lip in thought. How best to help him understand? "She's captain of the debate team and president of the science club, plus a bunch more clubs, *and* she's an athlete. You should see the flips she does with the cheer squad."

He stopped there, satisfied that he'd made his case.

Grandpa just shrugged. "And?"

Archie gave an exasperated laugh. "And, by every social math in the world, she's out of my league."

"You have your own talents. Has she read your stories? They're really good."

"She's also rich. Her parents are big, high-powered . . . uh, somethings. I forget what. Not that I care about the rich thing, but she might."

Grandpa gave a half-grin. "Have you asked her if she cares?"

"Well, I . . ." Archie stopped. They both knew he hadn't even asked her something simple, like whether she'd had a good weekend, much less what she would look for in a boyfriend. Assuming she was interested in having a boyfriend at all.

21

"Don't get me wrong, you're far from the first kid to get nervous over a crush. Happens to just about everyone."

"Not you, though."

"Of course, me," Grandpa said. "I'm not made of steel, Fletch."

"But . . . you fought in a war."

"And asking your Grandma Ella on our first date was still the scariest thing I ever did."

A twinge of pain crossed Grandpa's face, like it always did when he mentioned Archie's grand-mother. They had been inseparable right up to the day she died five years ago.

Archie still doubted. He couldn't remember ever seeing Raymond Reese afraid of anything.

"All right," Grandpa said. "You know how I like to tell you little life secrets now and then? Well, I've got another one." He leaned closer. "There are no leagues, Fletch. Only people."

Archie scoffed.

"Trust an old man—it's true. How do you think your grandma and I got together? Everything I was, she was better. And plenty of guys who were smarter and richer than I was wanted to date her. But they treated her like something they wanted to win, and

I just treated her like a person. We talked, joked, got to be real friends. And eventually, I asked her on a date. It was scary, but I just told myself I had a chance and tried to believe, and it worked. That's how people are, Fletch. Love isn't like applying for a job. It's not about facts or logic or status. If you want this girl to see you—I mean *really* see you—don't talk to this." He tapped Archie's head. "Talk to this." He tapped Archie's heart.

Archie leaned back in his chair, chewing on the advice. For someone who'd lived a life like Grandpa's, it made sense that he would look at love with a sense of adventure. For someone like Archie, who hadn't seen the world, who hadn't faced down mortal dangers and lived to tell the tale, could it work that way?

Before he could decide how he felt, Mom beckoned to Grandpa. Her eyes were heavy.

"Guess they're ready for me," Grandpa said. "You'll be okay out here?"

"Sure," Archie said, projecting as much confidence as he could.

From Grandpa's expression, it was obvious he didn't buy the calm facade. His eyes softened. "All for one."

"And one for all," Archie replied, finishing the quote from *The Three Musketeers*.

He was surprised to find it actually helped a little. Grandpa had bought that book for him when he started junior high, and he'd already read it multiple times. Once, they'd even read it out loud together. It was still one of Archie's favorites.

Grandpa joined Mom and they disappeared behind a large door with a nurse. Heaviness sat in the pit of Archie's stomach, threatening to pull him through the floor. He clung to Grandpa's voice for support, using their conversation like a life vest.

It'll be okay, he kept repeating to himself. *He'll be fine. Nothing to stress about.*

After repeating it two hundred times, he started to believe it a little. As the long minutes ticked by, his stomach slowly recovered. Of course everything would be okay. Raymond Reese had survived war and raging fires and falling buildings—a little forgetfulness was nothing.

The door opened. Mom and Grandpa appeared. Archie perked up, ready to hear the good news, the *don't worry about it* diagnosis. Then he saw their eyes.

His stomach dropped again.

Oh, no.

Chapter 3

Alzheimer's was unpredictable, so the doctors wouldn't say how long Grandpa could live a normal life. Some people lasted a year, some lasted ten. The only specific thing they had said was that Grandpa's condition seemed to be advancing faster than average.

Which meant that sometime in the near future, he would forget his family, his past, everything that made Raymond Reese the man he was. The disease had already been stealing those memories for months, and it wouldn't stop until they were all gone.

The ride home was quiet. Dinner was even quieter. Then everyone went to bed early.

Or at least they had gone to their rooms. Unable to sleep, Archie finished another book and went to get a drink. Now, as he returned from the kitchen, he spotted strips of light under both Mom's and Grandpa's doors.

There was a faint whispery sound coming from Grandpa's door that Archie had come to recognize as paintbrush on canvas. Grandpa had taken up painting when Grandma Ella died, and now he went back to it whenever he was stressed. Apparently he couldn't sleep either.

After closing his door, Archie flopped down onto his bed. The phrase *no known cure* wouldn't stop rattling around inside his head. All he could do was lie there, wondering. Worrying. What if Grandpa forgot all the good memories but remembered all the bad ones? Did that happen to people?

One of Archie's own memories resurfaced. A bad day from a few years back. Bad because Grandpa had been upset, and because Archie had been the cause.

The source of Archie's love for reading and writing was no mystery. He had grown up with books in his hands because Grandpa loved them and made sure they were always around. His passion for stories was contagious, so Archie was hooked from the day he learned to read.

As Archie grew, he and Grandpa would read the

same books and talk about their favorite parts. And slowly, over many books, discussing transformed into creating. When they loved a book too much to just talk about it, they used the words on the page to weave a fantasy world, where they could live the adventure side by side. One day they would become Peter Pan and the Lost Boys, battling Captain Hook for the future of Neverland. Another day, they would become Edmond Dantes, escaping prison to exact revenge on those who tried to destroy him.

Until soon after Archie turned ten. They had read *A Wrinkle in Time* and then traveled across dimensions to save his mother. When they returned to Earth, Archie declared that he was now far too old to be playacting. All of this was kid stuff, and he wanted to start growing up.

Grandpa didn't get angry or ask why. He just looked sad. "Okay, Fletch," he had said after a moment of silence. "Whatever you need."

They hadn't spoken about it since then. But Archie never forgot that look on Grandpa's face, and he never stopped feeling guilty for putting it there.

Would Grandpa still remember that day? Archie hoped he wouldn't. Then he felt selfish for hoping that.

~~~

The next morning, Archie plopped down on the couch with a book, his eyes scratchy with fatigue. So many feelings were happening all at once that his brain seemed to have short-circuited, leaving him weirdly numb.

Maybe that was why he hadn't cried. Should he have cried? He didn't know. He didn't really feel sad. Just kind of like he was . . . floating. Unfocused.

Three knocks on the front door. Archie looked up from his book but didn't move. The door was almost never locked during daylight hours when someone was home; their guests would let themselves in.

The door swung open. Aunt Candace stepped inside, wearing her customary dark suit with a pencil skirt and high heels that never looked comfortable. Just like the high-priced lawyers on TV.

She was on her phone, as usual, and not exactly barking but definitely speaking strongly. Even as she moved, every strand of her hair stayed perfectly in place, like it was afraid of her. Setting her purse down, she moved into a corner to finish her call.

Her husband, Dan Kane, sauntered in behind

her. Sporting worn-in jeans with a flannel shirt and an easy smile, he seemed completely relaxed wherever he was. Basically the polar opposite of Aunt Candace.

"Hey, Archie," he said, flopping down on the couch. "How's it going?"

Archie tried to smile and only half-succeeded. Uncle Dan's own smile faded, as if he'd just remembered why they were here. They had driven from downtown St. Louis so the grown-ups could decide next steps about Grandpa.

Uncle Dan looked apologetic. "Sorry. I know this stinks."

"That's okay," Archie said. "It does stink, but I'm glad you guys are here."

Uncle Dan nodded. "We'll all just have to help each other through it. Personally, I plan to help with inappropriate humor. Like, you know how your Aunt Candace is super serious every minute of every day?"

"Um, yeah."

"Well, that's why I like to do this."

Standing, Uncle Dan stepped closer to Aunt Candace. When she looked over at him, he pointed at her, then at his own heart.

"I love you," he whispered, then proceeded to spin around her in the most ridiculous "sexy" dance Archie had ever seen.

Aunt Candace rolled her eyes and kept speaking into the phone. "Yes. We'll get the contract signed and sent by messenger."

Undaunted, Uncle Dan kept writhing and spinning, his arms flailing overhead.

"Well, if they want it sent electronically, they'll have to—"

Aunt Candace cut off, stifling laughter. Archie's jaw dropped. It was like watching the first crack form on the ice of a frozen lake.

"Um, they'll have to use the same secure document-sharing service we do," she managed to say.

Stop! She mouthed, swatting at Uncle Dan. But then she laughed when he leaned over backwards to gaze at her from upside down, shimmying the whole time.

Uncle Dan came back to the couch wearing a satisfied grin. Aunt Candace resumed her serious I'm-in-charge-here tone.

"It's a tough job," Uncle Dan said. "But someone has to do it."

Archie laughed. He wondered if Uncle Dan realized how true that was. Nobody else could make Aunt Candace laugh like that. Even Grandpa's efforts failed, so he particularly enjoyed watching Uncle Dan succeed.

Aunt Candace finished her phone call and turned toward them. "Hello, Archibald. Where's everyone else?"

"Upstairs. They'll be down soon."

"Good. I ordered lunch to be delivered in half an hour."

Archie's eyebrows rose. "Way out here in Ithaca? That must have been expensive."

Aunt Candace just shrugged.

"Don't worry," Uncle Dan said. "Her morning meeting probably paid for lunch *and* dinner."

Ithaca was an hour's drive south of St. Louis, and Archie's house was in the country even by Ithaca standards. Decades ago, Grandpa had purchased thirty acres and built this house on the most picturesque spot—a wide green meadow with a creek running behind it, and tree-covered foothills rising in the background.

An awesome place to grow up. Archie loved it. Someone like Aunt Candace, though, was always going to leave it behind for the shiny big city.

Mom came downstairs a few minutes later, followed by Grandpa. Everyone settled in the dining room, sipping tea and making small talk while they waited for lunch. And for one other person.

"Violet didn't make it?" Grandpa asked.

"She texted. She'll be here any minute," Mom said.

Aunt Candace rolled her eyes. "Violet's running late? What a surprise."

"Be fair, Candy," Uncle Dan said. "She might've run over a squirrel. Then she'd have to stop and hold a little squirrel funeral for it."

Everyone laughed except Aunt Candace. Dan was the only person allowed to call her Candy, but the rest of the family found it especially funny given that their last name was Kane. It was even funnier when someone reminded her that her maiden name, Reese, was also a type of candy.

Archie heard the front door open and close. The youngest Reese sister burst into the room, wearing long pigtails and an expression as bright as her sunflower-print dress.

"Are we laughing already? Great! Morning, Daddy. Morning, everyone!" She kissed them all before finding her seat and pulling a small container from her hemp-woven purse.

"I ordered lunch from Fantaisie Mais Faux," Aunt Candace said.

"That's French for *one shrimp is twenty bucks for some reason*," Uncle Dan said.

"Ooooh, um . . . sorry, sis," Aunt Violet said. "Doesn't that place use, like, a ton of animal products? I'm only eating conflict-free grains and vegetables these days. Pure body, pure mind. That's what Constance says."

"Constance?" Archie asked.

"This genius director of the play I'm in. She's really opened my eyes. You know?" Aunt Violet popped open the lid of her container and took a huge bite of some kind of sprout. "Oh, that reminds me! Would you call me Avis from now on when we're out in public? That's going to be my stage name. Constance says it's important to have a name that aligns with my professional goals."

"You mean no-budget local theater and waiting tables at Applebee's?" Aunt Candace said.

"I mean pursuing artistic integrity," Aunt Violet said with exaggerated dignity.

"Isn't Avis a car rental agency?" Uncle Dan said.

33

"No, silly, it's Latin for *bird*."

"I'm pretty sure it's also a car rental agency," Mom said.

"You don't like the name we gave you?" Grandpa asked.

Aunt Violet frowned. "That's not it, Daddy. It's about expressing myself as an artist."

"Yeah, we're not calling you Avis," Aunt Candace said.

"But," Uncle Dan added, "we *will* call you if we need to rent a lightly used Honda."

Archie couldn't hold back his laughter anymore, and the rest of the family joined in.

Aunt Violet sighed dramatically, but she was smiling. "None of you normies get me."

The doorbell rang.

"That's lunch," Aunt Candace said.

Aunt Violet stood. "Art is forgiveness. So I'm going to answer the door for you and bring in the basket of cruelty you ordered. Even though you won't take me seriously."

When Aunt Violet had left the room, Aunt Candace shot an irritated look at Grandpa. "You and Mom just had to name her after a flower, didn't you? Now she thinks a name can be any silly thing."

"Candy Kane is right, names should be serious business," Uncle Dan said.

Aunt Candace shot him a look. Archie stifled his laughter.

"I would've thought you'd be happy to see her pick a new name," said Grandpa teasingly. "When she was born, you begged us not to name her after a flower. For some reason, you were convinced she'd end up an airhead."

"And I was so clearly wrong. Anyway, I won't apologize for having good taste."

"You just hate flowers," Grandpa said.

"Yeah," Mom added. "Even as a kid, you hated flowers. What little girl hates flowers?"

"Flowers smell up a room, and then they die," Aunt Candace said.

The mood turned sour in a blink. Archie watched the smiles fade, and that heaviness returned to the pit of his stomach as they were all confronted with the reason they were here.

This was really happening. They couldn't avoid it any longer.

"So." Grandpa laced his hands together on the table. "I guess we should talk."

Archie had fallen asleep on his face again. Rolling onto his back, he pushed away the pillow and scrubbed the sleep from his eyes.

After the family meeting, he'd collapsed into bed for a nap. Now, golden rays of late-afternoon sun filtered through the trees. He'd slept way too long and would probably be drowsy all evening.

The meeting had been a good thing for the grown-ups, though. Grandpa had announced he wanted as little medication as possible. He didn't want his last memories to be of horrible side effects.

In the end, it was decided that the family would help with whatever he needed and daily life would continue like normal for as long as possible. Eventually there would have to be nurses and pills. Just not yet.

This was real. Still, Archie didn't feel like crying. He just felt empty.

But he couldn't stay in bed forever. With a groan, he pushed off the bed and wobbled into the hallway. A little cold water on the face might help him shake off the nap.

At the far end of the hall, Mom's door was closed.

She must have been napping too, so Archie stepped quietly. Except his tired feet hit the one spot that always creaked. He winced but didn't hear anything behind Mom's door.

"Fletch?"

Grandpa's door was open. Archie crept inside to avoid more creaks.

Grandpa sat at his easel, which was next to the window looking out on the utility shed in the backyard, and the creek and the forested foothills beyond. His latest painting featured Grandma Ella, curled up in a chair and absorbed in reading a book. And not just any book—it was the Journal.

A framed photo of Grandma Ella sat nearby, next to the actual Journal, probably as references for the painting.

Archie thought of the Journal with a capital *J* because, in his mind, it was legendary. It contained stories of Grandpa's life as a younger man—a life full of adventure, dangers and challenges, travels around the world, triumphs and defeats.

Grandpa had been a soldier in Vietnam, then served as a firefighter for decades. In between, he had traveled the world, taking odd jobs to pay for his wanderings. He had been a bartender in Morocco, a coffee bean harvester in Guatemala, a wilderness guide in the Philippines, and more.

He had talked about some of his stories over the years, but not nearly all, and Archie had never been allowed to read the Journal. No one had been, except for Grandma.

Grandpa glanced over his shoulder. "Good nap?"

"I guess," Archie said. "Did you take one?"

"Nah, felt like painting. And a little reading." He tapped the Journal with his free hand. "Trying to remember as many of my own stories as I could. The good stories, anyway, the ones I'm proud of."

"I've heard your stories. What is there *not* to be proud of?"

Grandpa was quiet for a moment. Then he continued as if Archie hasn't spoken.

"I'm trying to keep the details as clear as possible, to hold onto 'em a little longer."

Archie didn't know what to say, so he just stood there. Eventually Grandpa put down his paintbrush and picked up the Journal.

"There's a story in here—your grandma's favorite. She asked me to read it to her a lot, at the end."

Sometimes Grandpa wanted to be alone with his thoughts. Archie got the feeling this wasn't one of those times. Steeling himself, he joined Grandpa at the window.

"Was it a story about her?"

"No, though there are plenty of stories about her in there," Grandpa said. "It was the apartment fire."

Archie nodded. Grandpa had been a rookie firefighter when an old apartment block went up in a blaze. No one had died that night, but someone would have if Grandpa hadn't been there. He'd heard a cry when no one else had and rushed back into an apartment that was engulfed in flames. It was how he'd gotten the burn scar on his left shoulder.

It was also how he'd saved a young mother and her little girl, carrying them out just before the building collapsed. Grandpa didn't tell his stories very often, but the people who really knew him never forgot that one.

For his work that night, he'd received the Medal of Valor. Archie glanced over at it, hanging on the wall in a shiny new frame. Grandpa had refused to display it for years—the job was never about medals, he'd always said—but recently Mom had convinced him to relent.

"Reading it always makes me think of your grandma," Grandpa said. "The way her eyes lit up when I first told her about it. The way she would look at me when I reread it to her—like I was her hero. She liked to imagine what that woman and her daughter had gone on to do with their lives. I don't want to forget any of that. Not until I have to."

Grandpa's eyes glistened. He swallowed before continuing.

"I can't help wondering, when will I forget her face? The sound of her voice? The scent of her perfume? Will they fade gradually, or will I wake up one day and they're just . . . gone?"

Archie's heart ached for his grandfather. A lot of men from his generation never took their armor off in front of anyone. They were expected to be tough all the time. Grandpa's armor was off now, and Archie wanted—needed—to help. But how?

His thoughts snapped back to those fantasies they had created together when Archie was younger. The worlds and the adventures they had shared. The joy it had brought them both. And Grandpa's sadness when it all went away.

Maybe I could try . . .

No. That was a silly thought. Trying to bring back a childish game would seem ridiculous.

Or it might work.

If it gave Grandpa even a moment of peace, wouldn't it be worth feeling silly? Wouldn't it be worth taking the leap and trying?

Archie grabbed Grandpa's arm and pointed out the window.

"There she is," he said. "Grandma Ella. See her through the trees, coming up from the creek? The grass has gotten tall again, and she's sweeping her hands through it as she walks. She loves the wildflowers when they bloom. Her hair is up, and she's . . ."

Archie faltered, emotion welling up to choke his words. What was he doing? This was all far too—

"She's wearing her yellow dress," Grandpa finished. "The one with little birds on it. She loves wearing it during summer. I love the way it catches in the breeze."

Just like old times—like they had never stopped doing it—the shared fantasy enveloped them. Archie sighed in relief as those old feelings rushed back. He could see everything now. Grandma Ella laughing as the dogs leapt and played around her, then catching sight of Grandpa and Archie in the window and waving. So full of life.

The smile on Grandpa's face warmed Archie's heart. He was seeing it too, filling the spaces in their fantasy with memories of the woman he'd loved and shared everything with.

Archie knew this feeling couldn't last; Grandma was gone. Even the dogs were gone. That didn't matter right now. What mattered was the peace Grandpa felt, and the comfort their fantasy brought him, even for a short while.

~~~

A few hours later, Archie sat on his bed reading. He didn't notice someone in his doorway until a throat cleared.

He looked up. "Oh, hey. My turn to make dinner?"

Grandpa stepped closer. Only then did Archie notice the odd look on his face and the object in his hand.

"I know you've always been curious, and I've always said no. But . . ."

Grandpa held out his hand, offering what he'd been carrying.

The Journal. It looked different now, with bits of labeling tape sticking out along the edges to mark certain pages. Reverently, Archie reached out and accepted the book.

"There are tough stories in here," Grandpa said. "About war and hard times. Decisions I still regret. Things I wouldn't want you exposed to. I only started writing them because a therapist said I should."

Archie held the Journal gingerly in his hands, feeling unsure about opening it now that he'd been given permission.

"I marked the good stories," Grandpa continued. "I trust you, Fletch. If you'll promise to only read those, you can read it whenever you like. Deal?"

Archie's voice was gone. Clutching the Journal, he nodded. He couldn't imagine a world where a Journal story could tarnish Grandpa's heroic past, but he agreed all the same.

"Good." With a satisfied nod, Grandpa turned to leave. Then he turned back. "Those stories are worth being remembered by someone, Fletch. If it can't be me . . . I'm glad it's you."

Chapter 4

"Nailed it again," Mr. Gertner said. "Nice job, Archie."

Archie grinned as the teacher handed back his paper. Most people groaned at essay tests, but he loved them. On-the-spot writing challenges were his Super Bowl.

Two weeks had passed since the diagnosis, and Archie hadn't realized how badly he needed a victory until he saw the big *105* at the top of his test. Reading and writing had been the only way to escape, even for a little while.

Zig got a B-minus. He looked at Archie with a smile and shrugged. "Good enough," he whispered.

Zig never stressed about tests—probably because he already knew his future. He would help run his family's restaurant empire once he graduated. It must be nice to have life figured out so early.

Archie stole a glance at Desta. She didn't look overjoyed, which probably meant her grade was similar to Zig's. Everyone knew her parents were laser-focused on academics. Archie suspected that they'd had high expectations for her since she was born—or maybe even before that, when the family had immigrated here from Ethiopia. They didn't take any test score lightly.

While the students looked over their results, Mr. Gertner stood by the whiteboard with his yardstick. Slicing it through the air, he made *snap-hiss-zhoom* sounds to mimic a lightsaber. A nerdy teacher, which meant he and Archie got along well.

"Man, this is ridiculous," Spencer Harrington said, pushing away his test. "Mr. G, why don't you just let us do multiple choice?"

The teacher kept slicing. "Life isn't always multiple choice, Spencer. In the real world, you'll need to know your stuff—sometimes at a moment's notice. If you don't know it, you'll need to fake it really well. You won't always get hints."

"Ugh." Spencer tapped Desta's arm. "So annoying, right?"

Archie tried not to bristle. Spencer never missed an opportunity to flirt with her. Desta's responses were always cryptic, so Archie couldn't tell whether she liked it or not.

Spencer loved attention, which was convenient since so many kids at school seemed happy to shower him with it. His rich parents were par for the course at Blue Sun, but he stood out for other reasons. He was tall and muscular—which explained why he was captain of the wrestling and baseball teams—with perfect hair and teeth.

Archie looked down at himself. He wasn't particularly tall or short. He wasn't the fastest or slowest. He could lose a few pounds, but he kind of liked that he'd inherited Grandpa's stocky frame. He was actually pretty strong. Taking care of land was a constant and physically demanding job, but the school didn't have a team for chopping wood.

Aside from that, his talents were all internal and hard to see. Plus, he didn't like being in front of people.

For someone like Desta Senai, who seemed to achieve anything she set her mind on, what kind of guy would stand out more? Archie wished he knew.

"All right," Mr. Gertner said. "put those tests away and focus up here, because . . . the time has come!"

Archie sat bolt upright. Expectant whispers exploded across the classroom. Everyone knew what

46

was coming. Eighth graders did it every year, and every year it was wildly different.

"That's right, folks, the Stone-Katzman Project," Mr. Gertner said in his fake broadcasting voice, clearly enjoying the drama. "You'll have the rest of the year to work on your topic. The last week of eighth grade, you'll all present at the gala . . . and it will be epic!"

People actually cheered, and their excitement wasn't fake. Everyone at Blue Sun looked forward to this. For the thousandth time, Archie reflected on how weird private schools could be.

Every eighth grader had to write an essay and do a presentation on the assigned topic, but the presentation could be pretty much anything, as long as it expressed some kind of "personal truth." Archie had seen kids do plays, interpretive dances, slam poetry, animation . . . and those were just the previous year. He felt his spirits rise. Finally, something he could dive into headfirst.

"Eighth graders, your assignment for this year's Stone-Katzman Project is . . ."

With a flourish, Mr. Gertner swung his yardstick and smacked one of the maps rolled up at the top of the whiteboard. The canvas unfurled to reveal not a map, but a banner.

"*Reach for the Future!*" The teacher smacked his yardstick on every word of the banner as he narrated. "High school is fast approaching. Before you know it, you'll be the adults running this planet. So, what are you going to be? What will you contribute to the world? Tell us in whatever way is *you*. You'll summarize your project in a three-to-five-hundred-word essay, telling us why it really matters to you. Other than that, there are no parameters. Be subtle, be flashy, be whatever you want. Just be true."

Smiles all around the classroom. A project with no limitations on how they could express themselves. Awesome.

"And this year . . ." Mr. Gertner held up his hand, signaling for quiet. "This year, you'll submit your essays four weeks before your final project is due. Five standout essays will be chosen, and if yours is one of them, you'll read it as a speech on project night!"

More excitement. The whole class seemed to be on board with this. Archie doubted that any Blue Sun students had made it this far without getting used to public speaking—the school made it part of the curriculum. And plenty of them would relish a little competition.

Staring at the banner, though, Archie found

his enthusiasm dragged down by anxiety. Because unlike his classmates, apparently, he had no idea what he wanted to be.

~~~

"Dude," Zig said, "we're going to ace this project. It's in the bag."

Archie gave a noncommittal shrug and opened his locker. "Hope so."

"It's perfect," Zig continued, opening his own locker. "I hope they're cool with open flames, because I'm gonna cook something ridonkulous! Seriously, your taste buds will explode."

Archie laughed. "That should be your project title."

"Hey, all great food should be a little dangerous. What about you? You don't talk much about what you want to do."

"Because I'm already a secret agent. They recruited me last year, I just can't talk about it." Archie narrowed his eyes at Zig. "And they'll know if you tell anyone."

Zig laughed. "I dare you to stand there in a suit and sunglasses, with just a bunch of blank posters behind you. When people ask about your project, put a finger to your ear and say *move along, sir.*"

"I'd get points for originality." Archie sobered. "Truth is, I've got no clue. So I'll need to make something up, or have some kind of dramatic realization in the next six months."

"Go for the realization thing. People love drama," Zig said. "We'll need to join a project group soon, but maybe we can get a head start tonight. Want to come over?"

"My mom's got a date tonight, so I'm supposed to hold down the fort while she's gone." Archie didn't add that *holding down the fort* really meant watching Grandpa in case he got confused. He still looked after himself for basic stuff, but a wave of disorientation could come out of nowhere at any time. So Mom didn't like him being left alone. "You can come to my place if you want."

Zig's grin faltered. "Oh, um . . . yeah, maybe. Let me check with my folks."

While Archie stuffed books into his bag, Zig pulled out his phone. His thumbs were a blur on the screen. He looked up just as Archie zipped his bag shut.

"Yeah, sounds good. I'll just ride home with you."

Zig moved to slip his phone back into his pocket,

and that's when Archie saw it. His friend had forgotten to lock the screen, giving Archie a glimpse of what he'd typed.

His insides turned upside down. "Come on, man. Really?"

"What?" Zig followed Archie's eyes to his phone screen. He winced. "Oh, no. Hey, bro, I didn't mean anything by it."

"You just searched *is Alzheimer's contagious*," Archie snapped, heat building in his chest. "If you don't want to come over, just say it."

"That's not it! I'm sorry, man. I didn't know how to ask without seeming like a jerk."

Archie hated his next words before he said them. "Well, you seem like a jerk anyway, so problem solved." He slammed his locker shut. "If you're so worried, don't come over."

"No, I want to—"

"I said don't."

Archie walked off before Zig could respond.

~~~

"That smells like heaven," Grandpa said, leaning over the sizzling pan. "What is it?"

"Your favorite," Mom said as she stirred. "Onions, potatoes, local farm sausage."

"It's my favorite?" Grandpa grinned. "I can see why. Can't wait to try it."

Leaning against the far counter, Archie watched the exchange. He saw as Mom looked up at Grandpa with a hint of sadness in her eyes.

"It's not quite ready, Dad. Why don't you go sit?"

"You're a good daughter," Grandpa said. "I should have had more."

Mom's stirring slowed. "Dad, you have three daughters."

Grandpa leaned back in surprise. "Truly?"

"Yes."

He laughed and gave her a hug. "Well, isn't that great news!"

As Grandpa left the kitchen, Mom's shoulders sagged. Archie watched her cook, feeling unequal to the job of trying to say something comforting.

"So," he said. "Not a great memory day, huh?"

He winced. That had been the exact opposite of comforting. It was true, though. There were still plenty of days when Grandpa was Grandpa. Then, without warning, there were days like this.

Mom shrugged. Then she surprised him by

52

laughing a little. "Not his best, that's for sure."

Archie moved to her side. "I can take over."

"Thanks. You'll need to keep stirring," she said, handing him the large wooden spoon. "You know how Grandpa likes it."

"Yeah."

He took her place and stirred, his mouth watering in anticipation.

Mom's high heels clicked as she walked to the far counter. Holding back freshly styled hair, she poured herself a glass of red wine and took a deep swallow. She always got nervous before dates, and this stuff with Grandpa wasn't helping.

"Where's John taking you?"

"Not John."

"Kyle?"

"Nope."

Puzzled, Archie peered at her over his shoulder. "Who, then?"

She sipped at the wine again before answering. "His name's Hal."

"I haven't met this one?"

"I don't think so."

"Huh." Archie turned back to the pan, his brow furrowed. "You've been going on, like, way more dates this month," he said. "Did you find a new spawn point or something?"

"A what?"

"Sorry, video game reference. Did you find some new place with new guys?"

He could hear the suppressed sigh in Mom's voice. "Just the usual places, Archie."

Great. Now this was a thing. He didn't care if she dated, and she knew that. But recently new guys were appearing at a notably higher rate than usual. It was odd, that was all.

"I'm not judging," he said. "Just curious. Everything okay?"

He watched over his shoulder as Mom stared at the floor, started to speak, then finished her wine instead. She set the glass down with a clink.

"Just look after Grandpa until he goes to bed, okay?" she said. With more clicking heels, she moved toward the living room and the front door.

"Mom, is Alzheimer's contagious?" Archie blurted. Then he gasped, mortified.

Mom whipped around, aiming a hard look at him. "Excuse me?"

"Well, um . . ." Archie swallowed hard. "I—I guess I've just been wondering."

Ever since Zig had asked—and he had reacted so badly—the question had been worming its way through his mind. Until it fell right out of his mouth.

Mom's hard expression wavered. Just a quiver of her bottom lip. A glistening of her eyes. Archie saw the truth then. She wasn't mad—she was struggling not to cry.

"No, it's not," she said, her voice tightly controlled.

With that, she spun around and went down the hall. He heard footsteps on the stairs. Then her bedroom door closed.

Archie tried to focus on finishing dinner and not on feeling like a complete jerk. Of all things to say without thinking, why did he have to say *that*?

Mom came downstairs twenty minutes later. Her makeup had been retouched, but he could see the redness around her eyes. She'd been crying. Because of him.

Before he could even apologize, she said a quick goodbye and left. Archie spent the evening playing checkers with Grandpa, answering the same questions Grandpa had asked that morning, feeling like the biggest jerk ever to walk the earth.

Chapter 5

Archie stood at his locker like a zombie, not quite awake, still trying to shake off the bleak mood of the night before. Moving sluggishly, he stifled another yawn and slid books for his first few classes into his bag.

Please let today be better.

When he closed his locker door, Zig was standing on the other side. He wore a triumphant grin.

"Who loves you?" he said.

Archie narrowed his eyes in suspicion. "Well, Mom always says I'm handsome, so . . ."

"Me," Zig said. "It's me and I just proved it."

"Um, how?"

"You know how everyone's making study groups for the Stone-Katzman Project?"

"Yeah."

"So. Friday at 4:30. Desta Senai's place."

". . . whoa." Archie blew out a breath and sagged against his locker. "You got us into Desta's study group?"

"Yeah, because I'm the best best friend ever." Zig glanced at the floor, his smile fading. "And because I was a total jerk yesterday."

"It's fine, Zig," Archie said. "I don't know how to deal with this, either."

Zig perked up. "Well, hey, now you get to hang with Desta Senai after school. Come on, tell me I'm not a genius. It's only happening once a month for now, but we'll meet more often as the due date gets closer."

Archie's insides quaked at the thought. What if he said something dumb? Or many somethings dumb?

But . . . wasn't it also an opportunity?

Archie tried to look serious, but Zig wasn't fooled.

"Aha! That's a win for Zig!"

~~~

After English, US history was his favorite class. At first that had been because of Mr. Gertner. Little by little, though, Archie had found himself growing more interested. The French and Indian War turned out to be surprisingly gripping.

The class was working in pairs to answer a set of questions on the latest chapter. The last section required a brief essay, so while Zig searched through the textbook to check their answers, Archie hunched over his laptop, typing as fast as his fingers could make the words.

He felt a presence as someone stopped between his desk and Zig's. Then his phone buzzed with a new message.

"My address for tomorrow," someone said.

Archie just nodded and kept writing, not really hearing the voice. He was in the zone.

"Awesome, thanks," Zig said. Then he bumped Archie's desk with his foot. Why was he doing that?

"So, what are you doing for your project?" the other person said.

Finally, the voice pierced Archie's bubble. He looked up to see Desta Senai gazing down at him.

He cleared his throat. "Um, me?"

Desta laughed. "Yeah, you. Everyone knows what Zig is doing."

"And how awesome I'll be at it," Zig said.

Desta laughed but stayed focused on Archie. They were finally having a real conversation, and of course it'd be over something he was completely lost about.

"Oh, well, you know that thing where you, uh . . . that one thing with the, um . . . it's kind of like . . ." Finally he deflated, giving up. "No, I don't know."

"Oh," Desta said. Did she seem disappointed? "Well, what do your parents do?"

"Mom's a dental hygienist. I never knew my dad."

"Sorry, I didn't realize . . ."

"It's fine. What about yours?"

"Well, my mom's a rocket scientist."

Archie laughed. Desta didn't.

"I'm serious," she said. "She works for Lockheed Martin."

"Oh. Wow, I didn't realize that was an actual job."

Desta was too nice to say how weird he was being. He could see it in her eyes, though.

"And my dad's a professor of rhetoric," she continued. "He teaches people how to form an argument."

"No wonder you're captain of the debate team."

She grinned. "I think he might've disowned me

if I wasn't. Anyway, maybe the study group can help you come up with something."

"Okay," Archie said. "Maybe I can return the favor—help people write their essays."

"Great idea. I sure could use it. And it'd be awesome if some of us made the top five."

Archie doubted that Desta would need any help, but she was sweet to say it. As for the top five, well, that was a distant dream for someone who didn't even know what to write about.

"Did you pick something yet?" he said.

She didn't hesitate. "Medical school. Surgeon, probably."

"Wow," Archie said. "You must be really excited about it."

Desta paused, looking confused. "Well, it's important, and it helps people. And my parents are serious about me being a doctor of some kind. So . . ."

Before she could finish, Kamiko Sato appeared.

"Yo, check it out," she said, handing her tablet to Desta. "He just put out a new one."

Desta's eyes went wide. She grabbed the tablet with glee.

"No way! Thanks, Kam."

What had gotten her so excited? Archie wanted to ask but stopped himself. Was it really his business? Desta probably already thought he was weird—he didn't want to seem rude on top of that.

Zig had no such fears. "Hey, what's that?"

Desta flipped the tablet around. "This amazing pencil artist I follow. The pieces take him forever to finish, so it's like a big event when he does."

"Wow," Zig said. "It looks like a photo."

"He's a genius," Desta said.

Now Archie remembered seeing her drawing. Sometimes at lunch, sometimes secretly during class while everyone else was taking notes. The way she lit up now, he could see how much she loved it. Yet she hadn't chosen it for her project. Interesting.

Desta turned toward Kamiko, rattling off her thoughts about the technique. It almost sounded like a foreign language.

Archie figured that signaled the end of their conversation. Which hadn't gone great, if he was being honest with himself. He must have seemed like a clueless underachiever to her.

She hadn't said that, of course. She was far too nice. But on the inside, wouldn't someone like her be thinking it?

Schmitty and Cobb were hilarious.

Archie lay on his bed, pillows piled high so he could sit up and read with the Journal open on his lap. He laughed again. Several entries Grandpa had marked were about Schmitty and Cobb, best friends who'd worked the same firefighting shift as Grandpa.

They loved playing pranks on the firehouse—especially when they could get the chief. This story was about the time they taped an air horn under the chief's adjustable seat. When he sat down, the horn went off, and he panicked so much that he fell out of his chair just as they burst in and snapped a picture.

Archie hadn't realized you could have fun with such a serious job. Still laughing, he turned the page.

"Schmitty and Cobb?"

Archie looked up to see Grandpa standing in his doorway.

"Yeah, the air horn thing. Those guys are the best."

Grandpa nodded. "Yes, they were."

Archie studied the page, trying to envision what the two men looked like. The only image he could conjure was one of legendary heroes, like dragon hunters in a fantasy. "Have you ever painted them?"

"Maybe I will sometime."

He was smiling, and there was something else behind his eyes. Archie couldn't tell what it was. Maybe just more old memories.

"So, how mad was the chief?"

"Not so mad about that one. He got pretty steamed a couple other times. Everyone knew he'd never fire 'em, though, so they kept playing pranks."

"Why wouldn't he fire them?"

"Because they were fearless."

"As fearless as you?"

"More. They never hesitated to charge into a fire, no matter how dangerous, if there was even a small chance to help someone. Those two saved a lot of lives." Grandpa's face took on a faraway look. "Including mine."

Archie sat up straighter. "I never heard about that. What happened?"

Grandpa started to speak, then hesitated. "Well, you'll get to it. It's in the Journal."

Wistfully, Archie said, "It'd be nice to feel brave like that."

"Hm. Something happen today?"

Archie flinched. He hadn't realized he'd spoken out loud. "Oh, just . . . I talked to Desta. Like, for real."

Grandpa brightened. "That's good."

"Not really. I was nervous and weird."

"Ever thought of telling her you're interested?"

Laughing, Archie set the Journal aside. "Or I could just toss my heart in a blender and let her hit *smoothie*."

Grandpa's expression turned pensive. "More and more, you talk like a little grown-up. You sure you're only thirteen?"

"Hey, it was your idea to send me to a fancy private school. This is what you get for your money."

"Good point." Grandpa chuckled, shaking his head. "Anyway, from the way you describe Desta, I doubt she'd be so mean."

"Yeah, I'm not worried about her being mean, exactly. But what if I try and she isn't interested, and then it makes everything super awkward and she doesn't even want to be friends?"

Grandpa sat on the edge of Archie's bed. "That might happen. Or she might respond how you hope. No way to know until you try. And no matter how it went, you'd still be a winner."

Archie scrunched up his face in doubt. "How?"

"Because you were afraid, but you did something anyway." Grandpa tilted his head, as if studying Archie. "You're stronger than you think, Fletch. I see it, and one day so will you. But until then, want another little secret about life?"

Archie nodded.

"We're all afraid. It's not just kids, it's adults too. We spend our lives too afraid of too many things." Grandpa's posture changed. Shoulders squared, chest high, eyes lighting up with an internal fire. "Sometimes, though, we fight the fear and win. We take the leap and make it to the other side. Sure, it doesn't always work out, but feeling defeated is better than feeling like we never tried. And all it takes is a few times to make a real difference, Fletch. A few brave moments can change your whole life. There are no guarantees. You just have to leap and hope you'll . . ."

His voice trailed off. Shifting, he glanced around the room, looking unfocused. Archie leaned forward, eager to hear Grandpa's next words.

But when their eyes met again, Archie knew something was wrong.

"Grandpa?"

Brow furrowed, Grandpa leaned away. The warmth in his eyes evaporated. He stared at Archie as if wondering why this strange boy was here.

Archie's stomach clenched. *No, please, not right now.*

"Schmitty and Cobb!" he blurted, desperate to keep Grandpa rooted in himself. To keep his memories flowing. "Tell me about what they did to the chief's chair."

"They . . . I, uh . . ." Grandpa began.

For one grand moment, Archie thought it had worked, that he had saved Grandpa from another episode. But then Grandpa stood abruptly and backed away toward the door.

"I should be going," he said. "Do I pay at the front desk?"

Archie's heart dropped into his stomach. "Um, no, that's okay. Bill's taken care of."

Grandpa gave him a wary look. "Oh . . . someone paid? All right, then. Suppose I'll check with the kitchen about dinner before I go."

The distrust in his eyes pierced Archie's heart, but he managed to fake a smile and a cheerful tone.

"Great idea."

Tipping an invisible cap, the shadow of his grandfather wandered down the hall. Archie collapsed back onto his pillows. Tears stung at the back of his eyes but refused to fall.

If only he could wave his hand and bring back the man he knew. If only there was some way to remind Grandpa who he was. To pull back those memories and . . .

Archie's eyes fell on the Journal. He froze, remembering how they'd envisioned Grandma Ella together—a combination of memory and fantasy that had not only brought Grandpa comfort but had helped sharpen his memories.

A desperate idea was taking shape in his mind. Why couldn't it work? And even if it didn't, what would he lose by trying?

Scrambling off the bed, Archie scooped up the Journal and barreled out of his room. He kept one eye where his feet were going and the other eye on the aged pages, frantically flipping through the stories that had been marked for him until he found the one he'd been searching for.

The perfect story, with an extra dash of fantasy from Archie, to bring the real Raymond Reese back.

Chapter 6

By the time Archie hit the ground floor, he had his plan. Snapping the Journal closed, he set it on the stairs, grabbed the banister, and swung around to dash down the hallway. He burst into the kitchen only seconds after Grandpa.

"Hurry!" he said, grabbing Grandpa's arm. "We can defeat it, but we have to go right now."

Grandpa stared at him. "Defeat what?"

"The beast that stole everyone's gold." Archie moved toward the back door, pulling Grandpa along. "Every gold piece is a part of us. It's like a memory. We have to get it all back, and only we can face that monster's fire!"

"Fire?" Grandpa snapped to attention. "Where?"

"Follow me. I tracked it outside the town."

"There's a town here?"

Archie didn't need to pull anymore. Grandpa followed him into the vast green backyard. Archie pointed toward the woods beyond.

"Yes, there's a town on the other side of the forest. See the buildings, just above the trees?"

Grandpa followed his gesture, eyes sweeping over the tops of the trees. Archie waited, trying not to look anxious. Hoping Grandpa would catch on and join in. If this didn't involve both of them together, Archie didn't think it would work.

But there was no spark in Grandpa's eyes, no recognition. He still looked like someone playing a game he didn't know the rules to. He was trying, but ultimately still lost.

Archie suppressed a sigh. Maybe he could figure out another way, try again tomorrow or—

"That stone roof," Grandpa said. "Is that . . . the duke's manor?"

A thrill raced through Archie. "Yes! The one that's all wacky angles. The duke who gave us this quest lives there."

With a rumble in the distance, the top of a building appeared beyond the forest, rising up from the ground fully formed: gray stone blocks and a steep roof topped with dark slate tiles.

Grandpa stared at their creation, his confusion transforming into a smile of wonder. "I see it, Fletch."

Archie felt like shouting in triumph. He forced himself to focus. These next steps would be crucial.

"Do you see the tower beyond it?" he said. "The one with the—"

"Huge bronze bell," Grandpa finished. "I see it, and the city walls."

"Yes!"

Another distant rumble and the tower appeared, its bronze bell gleaming in the sun. Massive city walls followed.

"They're so tall," Archie said. "Why would they have such tall walls? Maybe they had trouble with beasts before."

"Yes," Grandpa said. "Only this one is different because . . . because it can fly."

"And breathe fire."

"So it got past the wall, burned a few buildings . . ."

". . . raided the treasury while the people put out the fires, then flew off."

Smoke was rising in the distance now. Archie could smell it from where they stood.

"Which is why they sent for us," Grandpa said solemnly.

Archie nodded. "Because we're heroes. We eat danger for breakfast and look good doing it."

"Right you are, Fletch. Nice gear, by the way. Especially the cloak."

Archie glanced over his shoulder. His long cloak billowed in the wind. A soft gray accented by silver scrollwork, it perfectly complemented his leather armor and the ornate longbow slung across his back.

He nodded to Grandpa. "Same to you. No cloak, but that armor looks tough as nails."

"Time to put it to the test." Grandpa stalked forward like a hunter, heavy steel-plate armor clanking with every step. "We've tracked it across the farmland outside town."

Archie walked by his side, eyes roving back and forth in search of their prey. "Then off the roads and through the woods. We crossed over that stream."

The creek behind their house widened, crystal clear water rushing over river rock and under an ancient stone bridge.

"And then here," Grandpa said. "Foothills and meadowland, far as the eye can see."

Archie spun in a circle as they walked, appreciating the untamed beauty of the country that had sprung up around them. "It must've thought no one would be brave enough to chase it."

"But it didn't know about us."

Rounding the curve of a foothill, Grandpa stopped and pointed. There, half-hidden behind brush, was an opening in the side of the hill. Beyond it was blackness.

"That cave," he said.

"The beast is inside with the gold," Archie said.

Grandpa nodded. "I can smell it."

"If we move fast, maybe we can sneak by it and—"

Archie froze as a heavy thump shook the ground. Then another, louder this time, and the ground shook again.

Footsteps.

A beast the size of a sailing ship burst from the cave mouth. With an earsplitting roar, it spat a river of flame at the two adventurers.

"Dragon!" Archie shouted.

"Move!"

Grandpa shoved Archie one way and dove the other, barely saving them from being roasted. The dragon roared and stomped, great claws chewing furrows into the earth.

Archie hit the ground. In one smooth motion, he rolled back to his feet, longbow in hand. Drawing an arrow, he nocked it and pulled back the bowstring. He was just barely too slow.

"Watch out!" he called.

Grandpa spun in time to see the dragon dive straight at him. He drew a blade of shining steel and swung with all his might. The dragon screeched in agony as a cluster of its armored scales buckled. Then Grandpa's blade shattered into glittering pieces.

Rising up, the dragon curled until its smoldering mouth pointed down at Grandpa. It sucked in a breath, preparing to reduce him to cinders.

No time to aim properly—Archie trusted his instincts and released the arrow. It struck the dragon's flank and exploded in a plume of purple flames.

The dragon rocked to the side with a heavy grunt, then shot skyward, its massive wings beating the air. Soaring far out of their reach, it ascended until almost touching the clouds, then dove again. The wind screamed around its monstrous form as it hurtled like a missile . . . straight at them.

"That thing's fast," Grandpa said.

"We'll be ready," Archie replied.

Side by side they stood on the scorched earth left by the dragon, muscles tense as they watched the dragon's approach. As they waited for the right moment.

Archie felt a tremor of fear and squashed it. No one could do this but them, so one way or another, they were going to try. Even though the beast was fifty times their size and breathed bone-melting fire. Even though flight gave it an advantage they could never match and—

Wait. That was the answer. Unslinging his quiver, Archie tossed the bow and arrows to Grandpa.

"I have an idea, but we need to trade weapons. My bow for Winterheart."

Grandpa shot Archie an incredulous look.

"I know the sword is special to you," Archie said. "I'll look after it, I promise."

"What are you planning?"

Archie summoned his best roguish smile. "To go for a ride."

Grandpa nodded with approval and drew an object from a sheath at his waist. "Only press the jewel when you're ready."

He set the hilt of a sword in Archie's hands. An oval-shaped blue jewel glittered in the cross guard. Strangely, this sword had no blade, but Archie knew that was the key.

He could hear the flapping of leathery wings now. The dragon roared, shaking the trees with the power of its voice.

Archie glanced up. "Almost there."

Grandpa nodded. "Right. I'll keep it busy."

"Thanks."

He exchanged a silent salute with Grandpa. Then they sprinted in opposite directions. Just as they parted, the ground where they'd been standing burned under a jet of searing flames.

Reaching under his cloak as he ran, Archie slid Winterheart into his belt. Then he pulled out a grappler attached to a chain that wrapped around his waist.

The dragon swooped down in the wake of its flames, skimming the ground. As it flew between the two heroes, a purple explosion rocked it from the opposite side. Grandpa had loosed his first arrow and scored a hit.

Taking advantage of the distraction, Archie reversed direction and dashed straight at the dragon.

He flung the grappler and latched onto the tail just as the creature flew by.

The chain pulled taut with a metallic snap, and suddenly Archie was flying. The dragon angled skyward again with no idea what it was dragging.

Archie reached down to the little clockwork machine at his waist and smacked the button. With staccato clanks, the machine began to spin and retract the chain attached to the grappler. Bit by bit, he drew closer to the monster.

The wind whipped at his face as they flew. He blinked against it, trying to clear his vision, and caught his first sight of the ground below. *Far* below.

Fear flashed through him. He stomped it down, focusing on his task.

Archie stood now on the beast's thick tail. Unhooking the grappler, he looped it back onto his belt and began climbing up the heavy spines along the dragon's back.

The dragon brushed the bottom of a cloud. For an instant it paused, hovering at the apex of its flight before turning back toward the ground. For that glorious instant, Archie floated weightless. He savored the rush, the moment stretching on in his mind.

The dragon dove hard toward Grandpa, who

faced the next attack alone. Archie barely held on, his stomach leaping into his throat as they careened toward the earth. He gritted his teeth and resumed climbing. Forward another step, past another spine. Then another. Then another.

The ground loomed closer.

Grandpa loosed arrow after arrow, their impact creating purple explosions that kept the dragon preoccupied.

Archie leapt with all his might. He flew forward, landing on the dragon's neck.

One of the dragon's huge eyes rotated and caught sight of him. It roared in rage.

Dropping to his knees, Archie drew the grappler, cocked back his arm, and let it fly. With a flick of his wrist, the chain wrapped around the dragon's neck and swung back around to Archie. He snatched the grappler from the air and hooked it to his belt.

Now the dragon was bridled like a horse. With an angry bellow, it twisted into a barrel roll, spinning until Archie couldn't see straight. Only the grappler chain kept him from flying off.

They were seconds from colliding with the ground. Grandpa was counting on Archie to finish this.

Drawing Winterheart from his belt, Archie gripped it in both hands and pressed the blue jewel in the cross guard. The air around it hissed and swirled and condensed until a blade appeared where there was none before.

A blade of pure ice.

Summoning all his strength, he plunged the blade through the back of the dragon's neck and into the base of its skull. The great monster shuddered and gasped, spitting a burst of flame. The flame turned to steam, and then to frost.

Steam jetted from the creases in the dragon's scales. Its body went limp.

With bone-shaking force, it plunged headfirst into the hillside, carving a deep furrow in the earth. Archie felt an explosion rock the entire hill, as if triggered by the dragon's demise. When the dust cleared, Archie looked up.

And grinned.

Gold coins fell from the sky, blown out of the dragon's cave by the explosion. Like molten rain-drops they hit the ground all around Grandpa. He had fallen onto his back, but he was laughing with pure joy and clutching fistfuls of treasure.

Laughing himself, Archie closed his eyes and

kissed Winterheart in gratitude. Now that the treasure had been recovered, Grandpa could—

"What on earth is going on here?!"

The angry voice pierced the bubble, invading the fantasy Archie and Grandpa had built. The wild countryside suddenly unraveled to reveal the real world.

Archie sat on the peak of the utility shed's roof—their "dragon." The pointed stick that had been in his hands was now protruding from one of the roof's broken shingles. Grandpa sat on the ground next to the shed, the grass around him littered with pocket change.

Mom was home early. She rushed toward them, glaring up at Archie as she knelt by Grandpa's side.

"Come down this minute, Archie. What do you think you're doing? Dad, are you okay?"

For an instant that felt like eternity, Grandpa gazed up at his daughter.

Please let it have worked. Please.

"Lighten up, Penelope." Laughing, Grandpa climbed to his feet. "Fletch and I were just having an adventure."

Archie breathed a sigh of relief. Grandpa's eyes were clear and aware. Squeezing Mom's hand in a conciliatory gesture, he looked up at Archie.

"You wanted to hear more about Schmitty and Cobb?"

Archie nodded eagerly.

"Climb down and we can talk over dinner." Grandpa looked to Mom. "That okay with you?"

Mom tried to maintain her stern expression, but it couldn't hold up against their joy.

"You two are total goofballs. You know that, right?" Shaking her head, she pointed at Archie. "You're fixing that roof, young man."

Archie nodded, grateful to have escaped real punishment. He climbed down and joined his family as they walked toward the house.

Where a man in a sport coat waited. "Um, everything okay, Penny?"

The three of them stopped.

"I totally forgot he was coming," Mom whispered. "We're supposed to go to dinner."

Another new guy? Archie squashed that thought before it could find its way to his mouth.

"Sorry, James," Mom called. "Just had to check on my guys. I'll be ready in a minute."

Archie tried, but he couldn't resist. "Hey, James, want to try some dragon meat? It's fresh!"

James eyed them all as if wondering what world

he'd wandered into. "Um, maybe I'll just wait in the car."

As soon as he was gone, Archie and Grandpa burst into laughter. Mom tried again to be stern but wasn't very convincing. "Oh, what am I going to do with you two?"

Archie wasn't worried. Because for tonight, Grandpa was himself again.

His plan had worked.

Chapter 7

Nothing could touch Archie today. He was flying high.

Grandpa had spent the rest of yesterday being himself. His real self that Archie had so many memories of growing up with. Like he wasn't even sick at all. It had carried through to this morning at breakfast, which put the whole family in a great mood. Mom had practically danced out the door on her way to work.

Archie breezed through his classes, aced a pop quiz in science class, made everyone laugh with a clever grammar joke in English, and nailed every US history question Mr. Gertner threw his way.

It was good to feel so invincible.

Even Spencer Harrington couldn't bring him down. Not even when he pulled up his sleeve and literally started flexing in front of Desta. Archie just shook his head and floated by, pitying the guy's shameless need for attention.

Then came the cherry on top. It was Friday, which meant the first meeting of the project study group was happening at Desta's house.

Zig's mom dropped them off near the driveway. Archie took in the scene as he got out of the car. Long, curvy driveway lined with manicured hedges. Beautiful front yard with geometrically perfect flower gardens. Giant red brick house with white trim.

Flawless. Any other day, Archie might have felt intimidated.

But not today.

The front door swung open and there she was, wearing a yellow sundress and a smile so bright it lit up the neighborhood.

"Hey, guys," Desta said, beckoning them inside. "Glad you could make it."

The boys greeted her and followed her to the dining room, where they found plush chairs circling a huge antique table.

Kamiko Sato was already there. They all said hello and sat down.

"Snacks and drinks are in the kitchen, so help

yourself." Desta sat, legs folded beneath her on her chair. "I can't wait to hear everyone's plan. Kamiko wouldn't tell me hers until everyone got here."

"Four people," Zig observed. "Good, a small group's better."

"Actually, there's one more coming," Desta said.

"Who?" Archie asked.

At that moment, they heard the front door open and close.

"All right, I'm here, so now it's a party."

Despite his current invincibility, Archie felt his smile droop. *Oh, come on. Really?*

Spencer Harrington plopped down on the fifth chair. Captain Perfect had changed from the regular shirt he'd been wearing at school into a skintight tank top. A tank top in October.

"Who has two thumbs and is going to ace this project?" He pointed his thumbs at his own chest. "This guy."

A grandfather clock chimed four o'clock. Desta sat up straight and folded her hands on the table. Suddenly she was all business.

"Should we get started?" she asked, though it didn't come out like a question. "We know how important the Stone-Katzman Project is. You're all smart and talented, and I think we can help each other make the best projects ever."

"Got that right," Kamiko said. "And we've got a secret weapon helping us with the essays. Right, Arch?"

"I'll do my best," Archie said, but he could feel his untouchable mood wavering. Somehow this project had managed to sneak right past his armor and hit him in the chest.

At least we don't have to choose something yet.

"Let's start by going around and sharing what our project is going to be," Desta said.

Oh, great.

"I'm obsessed with animals. Definitely going to be a vet," Kamiko said. "No clue what I want to say in the essay, but I've already got a vision for my booth setup. It's going to rock."

"Let me guess—petting zoo?" Zig joked.

"Close! I'm gonna partner with animal shelters and run a pet adoption drive right there at the exhibit hall."

"Kam, that's awesome!" Desta said. "It's clever and original. I love it. Zig?"

"Culinary school and restaurant management— no big shock. But I'll have a surprise." Zig leaned forward, bursting with eagerness. "I'm creating a new ramen recipe, a fusion of Japanese and Hawaiian ingredients, with my own special twist. I'll make and serve it from my booth. I'm even going to sear scallops over a live flame to add to each bowl."

"Nice!" Archie said. "Dinner and a show."

"Will you make some for us?" Kamiko said.

"Oh, you're going to be my taste testers. I have to get it just right. As for the essay, I'm not sure yet, but we've got time."

Spencer frowned. "Is ramen fatty? I don't wanna pork out."

Before he could stop himself, Archie scoffed. "Can't you just run an extra mile?"

"I could," Spencer returned. "And you should."

Any other day, that would have cut him. Today, Archie just grinned.

"Come on, Spencer," Desta chided. "You know you'll eat it and love it, so stop fronting."

That shut him up. Archie's grin widened.

"I'm still going with surgeon, of course," Desta continued. "Not sure how to present it and make it fun, though. Pictures of surgery would probably kill the mood."

Archie remained surprised at her choice. She

seemed so mechanical when she talked about it—there was no excitement behind her eyes. Still, maybe there were deeper reasons he didn't understand, and as he'd reminded himself before, it wasn't his business anyway. In any case, he wanted to help.

"We can brainstorm with you," he said. "There must be something you could show that would draw a crowd. Some kind of mock demonstration, maybe."

Desta nodded. "Thanks, that's a good start."

"I want to hear what Big Arch has planned for himself." Spencer crossed his arms and leaned back with a smirk. "Gonna write us a poem?"

Archie didn't seethe or retreat. Not this time. "Actually, yeah, it's called An Ode to the Disaster That Is Spencer's Face. Want to hear it?"

Zig, Desta, and Kamiko burst out laughing.

Archie braced himself for retaliation. He'd never come back at Spencer like that before, and someone with that guy's ego wouldn't—

Spencer laughed. "Good one."

Wow. He took a joke.

"You're sticking with what you chose?" Desta asked Spencer.

"Get by on good looks and charm? Yep."

Desta gave him a long-suffering look, and Spencer held up his hands in surrender.

"Yes. Same thing I told you before."

"Which is?" Kamiko said.

Professional baseball player, probably. Or professional owner of a baseball team. That would be a natural fit, considering that Spencer's parents had donated most of the Blue Sun team's budget. Archie would have bet every dime in his embarrassingly small savings account that Spencer would go for something that got attention.

"There are these big charity foundations," Spencer said. "They have boards of directors that decide how they spend the money—like what people or causes to help. Figure I can do something like that. Plus, I can kick in some cash, and they wouldn't even have to pay me."

"Whoa," Zig said. "How will you do it for free?"

"Oh, my parents set up a trust for me." Spencer waved his hand dismissively. "Long as I don't buy like a dozen mansions, I can live off it pretty much for life. Besides, you know someone's gonna ask me to model their fancy underwear. Pretty sure that pays."

Classic Harrington, thought Archie. He'd picked an idea that would make him look generous without requiring him to do any actual work. It felt too early in the process to say anything critical, but secretly Archie couldn't help judging. Throwing money at a problem didn't make someone a good person. Lex Luthor did that all the time in the comics, and it didn't stop him from trying to kill Superman every month.

"So, Archie, what *are* you doing?" asked Kamiko.

"Oh, that's okay, we don't all have to share yet," Desta cut in with a glance at Archie.

Which only made him fall harder for her. She must be thinking of their discussion in class and trying to save him from embarrassment.

"No, it's okay. I haven't picked one yet. I just . . . well, how can I know what I want to be for the next fifty years?"

"Just pick *writer* and sit in your booth typing all night," Spencer said.

Archie nodded. "I might. Or I could teach you how to read."

Everyone laughed again—even Spencer. *Wow, Invincible Archie's great with comebacks.*

"Anyway," Archie went on, "there are lots of different kinds of writers, and I probably couldn't be, like, a science journalist and a novelist at the same time. Or maybe I could, but I don't know how to make that happen. I mean, I'm only thirteen. How am I supposed to have all this figured out?"

"I get it," Desta said. "High school lasts four years. That's a long time. Who knows how we might change by the end of it?"

Archie felt himself smile, and amazingly, she smiled back. They broke eye contact before it got weird, though.

One by one, they helped each other dive into their projects. Desta had gotten each of them a folder with scrap paper and a fancy pen from the university where her dad taught, so that everyone could take brainstorming notes. Archie drew no closer to finding his subject, but it was satisfying to help his partners.

When it was time to leave, Desta leaned across the table to talk to Kamiko in a low voice. She opened another folder and took out a sheet of paper to show Kamiko.

While she spoke in an animated undertone, the folder sat open on the dining table, and Archie caught a glimpse of the contents: pages and pages of drawings. Everything from sunflowers and mountains to spaceships and robots.

They were amazing.

~~~

The smells wafting from the oven made Archie's mouth water. Sitting at the kitchen table, he tried to ignore them and focus on his project notes. Multiple pages were crisscrossed with a thousand scribbles. A few phrases were circled, but most were already crossed out.

Writer—that was the easiest answer. Specifically, novelist. Archie loved writing and suspected that he always would. Especially when he combined classic old stories with newer ideas, or even real-life experiences, to create something fresh and unique. But did he want that to be his whole life, for the rest of his life? Deep down inside—that place where there should have been some instinct about the right answer— there was an echoing void. A whole lot of nothing.

The oven door squeaked as Mom opened it and pulled out a piping hot pizza. Very high heels clicked across the floor as she brought it over to cool on a countertop. Those shoes could not be comfortable. Archie had told her that he could make dinner and that she should focus on getting ready for her date, but Mom had wanted to make sure her guys were fed before leaving.

She seemed oddly anxious. Now that Archie thought about it, she had been that way about the last several dates. This time it was just more obvious. He wondered why.

Since Archie's father had never been around, dates were just a natural part of Mom's life. In the past, she'd always been super casual about it. Sometimes she dated, sometimes she didn't. Most of the time she seemed okay, whether she ended up in a relationship or not.

Now the air around her felt different, and the more anxious she grew, the fancier her date outfits became. Archie wasn't sure why things were changing, and it felt weird to bring it up. So he just hoped Mom would be able to relax again soon.

Leaning over the pizza, she inhaled. "Mmm, sausage and mushrooms. I'm jealous."

"You can have some, you know. You made it."

"No garlic breath on dates. It's an unspoken rule. And I already brushed my teeth."

"You brushed your teeth *before* going to dinner?"

Mom paused as if she hadn't considered how odd that was. "Well . . . first impressions are important."

"Dating is weird, right?"

"People are weird. So, yeah."

She went about slicing the pizza into wedges, heedless of the danger it presented. Standing, Archie moved to the counter and gently pried the slicey wheely thing from her hands.

"You want to get sauce on your dress? Let me do it."

Mom tousled his hair affectionately. While he sliced, she pulled a mirror from her purse and triple-checked her makeup.

What do you want to be?

The question bounced around his head like a song that wouldn't quit playing. If he could choose literally anything, what would it be? Would life or the universe or whatever even let him follow a dream? He'd seen enough to know things rarely worked that way.

As he made the final slice, he glanced over at Mom. She had finished her checkup and stared into space now, lost in thought.

Life certainly hadn't happened the way young Penelope Reese had planned. Right after college, she had moved to New York City to work on Wall Street—the fast-paced world of stocks and trading and other stuff Archie didn't understand. She had lived for it.

Then came a marriage—sudden, disastrous, and over in a blink—to a guy who didn't even stick around for Archie's birth. For the first time now, Archie found himself wondering . . .

"Do you ever regret leaving New York?"

Mom's head whipped toward him. "No! Why would you ask that?"

"Well . . . I mean, you had big plans. Then things happened and you wound up raising a kid in the middle of nowhere." He shrugged. "Wasn't it, like, the opposite of what you wanted?"

Mom looked pained. "I hope I've never made you feel that way."

"No. I just wondered, with this project and everything."

Mom looked into his eyes. "When it comes to you, I don't regret anything for one second."

"But it couldn't have been easy."

"Was it an adjustment? Of course, and sometimes I wonder what might've happened if certain things had been different. But the moment I first held you, I knew what I was going to do and I never looked back."

"Why? I mean, how? Or, I guess, both."

Mom paused, pondering. "When they put you

in my arms, everything changed. I looked into your eyes and it was like I saw the next twenty years. Living in the big city with a job that kept me working all hours, never home, always stressed. You'd grow up without a parent around. Suddenly, what I had wanted before seemed so . . . trivial. I loved my job, but it didn't hold a candle to how much I loved you."

Archie began to understand. "So you moved back home, where you could . . ."

"Start over and build the life I wanted for us. I went back to school and picked something that would let me be home for dinner every night."

"No regrets, then? Not even one?"

Mom seemed to look inward, her expression soft. "Raising you in this beautiful place, watching you have all this time with your grandparents— especially your grandfather—and seeing you growing into a good man like him . . . those memories are priceless, Archie." Mom reached out and took his hands. "No big city could ever match them. Do you believe me?"

He really did. Smiling, she pulled him into a tight hug—awkward but heartfelt with the counter stuck between them.

"This probably looks ridiculous for anyone not currently hugging," Archie said.

"Aw, that's their problem."

They laughed together.

Someone cleared their throat. They turned to see Grandpa standing in the kitchen doorway, wearing a full suit and a fedora. He clutched the handle of an old suitcase.

Archie stiffened. So did Mom. From the look in Grandpa's eyes, they knew what was coming before he spoke.

"You have a fine establishment," Grandpa began. "But we should be heading on home now. My, uh . . ."

He turned in a circle, looking puzzled.

"My wife must be in the car." He patted pockets with his free hand. "Have we paid you?"

They had tried different ways of handling these situations. Some worked, some failed utterly, and sometimes a tactic that had been helpful once had no impact the next time. Every day was uncharted territory. So, how should they handle this one?

Mom stepped forward and held out her hand. "Of course. Let us help you with your bags, make sure you've got everything packed."

So they were playing along today. Archie crossed his fingers that it would work. He tried to breathe normally. Steady, in and out.

Grandpa leaned back, eyeing Mom as if unsure he could trust her. Then he seemed to decide in her favor and handed over the bag. Mom lifted it onto the table and unzipped it.

"Let's see what we have," she said, drawing out each object she found. "A hammer. A wooden hanger. Half a loaf of bread. And a book."

Archie came to Mom's side, ready to lend support. The air around her vibrated with tension. She stared down at the items Grandpa had packed, as if caught between two paths. Her eyes welled with tears. Her lip was quivering . . .

Mom burst into laughter. As it poured out, Archie saw the tears retreat. The tension shattered like glass, and suddenly they were both laughing so hard that they had to lean on each other for support.

Grandpa watched them, puzzled at how oddly these strangers were acting but too polite to call them out on it. Eventually Mom recovered enough to close the suitcase and hand it back.

"You've paid, but dinner is included," she said.

"How about you wait in your room and we'll bring it to you?"

Grandpa smiled and tipped his hat. "I suppose that'd be okay. Ma'am. Sir."

He turned and walked back down the hall. They heard his footsteps on the stairs.

The quiet moment gave Archie time to reflect. From the outside, anyone who saw what had just happened might think he and Mom were callous or uncaring. They might see all the mistakes, all the reasons why what they'd done seemed wrong.

If you haven't been there, you can never know what it's like.

That's what he would tell them. As time went on, and the scale weighing good days and bad started tipping in the wrong direction, sometimes you had to let the absurdity of it all wash over you. You had to turn the steam valve, release the tension.

Because on those days, the only thing you could control was how you reacted. Sometimes you reacted with tears, and that was okay. But if you never chose to laugh, those days would destroy you as surely as the disease. If Grandpa had the choice, Archie knew he would have chosen for them to laugh, even if only for a moment.

"Great," Mom said. "Now I have to leave a chocolate on his pillow tonight."

They burst into laughter again.

"He'll probably forget and be okay in an hour." Mom wiped mirthful tears from her eyes, no longer seeming to care about her makeup. "But I can cancel the date if . . ."

"No, you should go," Archie insisted. He was thinking about the book that had been in the suitcase. The Journal. He knew exactly how to help Grandpa. "Don't worry, we'll be fine."

Chapter 8

The idea came from an entry in the Journal. In Grandpa's twelfth year as a firefighter, there had been a huge forest fire in Arkansas, several hours away. Huge enough that firefighters from a wide area were brought in to help.

Grandpa and his company arrived just after another company got trapped in a dangerous position. So the fire department sent air tankers to drop flame retardant and make a path, then sent helicopters carrying Grandpa's team to rescue them.

When Archie read the story, it felt like he was right there with Grandpa, flying toward danger to save lives. An incredible feeling.

That was how he ended up here—soaring through the sky like he had with the dragon. This time was different, though, because he wasn't the passenger. He was the flyer.

Puffy white clouds raced by below him. Cold wind ruffled his hair, and he adjusted his goggles to keep it from stinging his eyes. It was almost time.

Archie dropped his left arm a few inches and swooped to the left. As he turned in a wide, sweeping arc, the leathery wings and bone harness creaked. He tightened the straps across his chest, securing them against the scales covering his torso.

His new flying apparatus came courtesy of the dragon he and Grandpa had vanquished. Once, it had tried to take them down. Now its wings, bones, and scales would help them rescue their friends from the island where they were held captive.

But wings couldn't get them all the way to their destination. Which was why their first target was . . . *there*. The clouds parted and Archie caught sight of a ship. With three tall masts and sails unfurled, it was slicing its way swiftly across the open sea.

A shadow whooshed by overhead. Cutting from right to left, it came alongside with Archie and matched his speed. He looked over at his grandfather, who wore a similar dragon wing apparatus. They saluted each other.

Then they dove hard.

Folding back his wings, Archie zoomed downward, Grandpa at his side. They left the cloud layer behind. In seconds, the wind grew warmer and the sailing ship seemed to multiply in size.

Adrenaline surged through Archie's veins like a beautiful fire. He let himself enjoy the dive, shouting in exhilaration as they sliced through the air. A hundred yards above the water, they redeployed their wings and leveled out, flying parallel with the water now.

The sound of a warning bell echoed across the water. Someone on the ship had spotted them, and now they were calling everyone on deck to defend.

Good. This was why they had approached during the day. They wanted the crew's attention.

These weren't just sailors. The Jolly Roger flag flying at topmast confirmed what Archie had suspected about them. Pirates.

BOOM!

The air shook. The sky around Archie and Grandpa filled with exploding cannonballs. But no ship gunner was fast enough to track them. They swooped and twisted around missiles like this was a toddler's obstacle course.

Finally, they landed on the prow of the deck, Archie on the starboard side and Grandpa on the port side. Keeping their wings half deployed, they waded into battle.

Screaming pirates came at Archie in waves. He moved through them like a tornado, ducking and spinning and leaping between the flashing steel of their weapons.

His bow was a whirlwind in his hand. One second he wielded it like a staff, batting aside cutlass blades. The next second he loosed a barrage of arrows, blasting the pirates overboard with purple explosions. Each enemy he vanquished puffed into smoke and disappeared.

Step by step he advanced across the deck. When he reached amidships—halfway to their goal—he paused for an instant to glance port side.

Grandpa was relentlessly swinging Winterheart's icy blade. The pirates who didn't freeze and shatter ended up tossed overboard and left behind in the ocean.

Grinning, Archie turned back to his own fight and loosed another wave of arrows. His enemies were falling faster now as he built up momentum.

Before he knew it, he was at the back steps

leading up to the stern. Grandpa tossed the last of his foes overboard and joined him at the helm.

Where the pirate captain waited.

Holding the giant wheel, the captain wore a relaxed smile. Like it didn't even bother him that two intruders had reduced his crew complement to zero.

"Not bad," he said.

"We're not finished," Archie said.

"That a fact?"

"It is," Grandpa said. "We'll be taking that wheel now. You can take a lifeboat."

The captain shrugged. "Oh, don't have any. Never was a fan o' lifeboats. Why give a crew a way to escape, when they should be bringin' me gold?"

"You mean that crew?" Archie gestured to the empty deck.

The captain chuckled. "The lads were never goin' to survive today anyway. None of us are."

Grandpa took a step forward. "Explain that."

"Don't have to." The captain nodded over Grandpa's shoulder. "See for yourself."

Archie turned and peered ahead of the ship. Then he saw it.

While they were fighting the crew, the captain

had turned them toward a furious whirlpool in the middle of the sea. At least ten times the size of the ship, it could easily swallow them whole.

"Hope ye made peace with whatever god ye worship," the captain said. "I'm sendin' us down to oblivion."

Archie knew this place now. It was the home of a watery beast that fed on passing ships and their sailors. He stared at the vortex, then exchanged a look with Grandpa. They both burst into laughter.

For the first time, concern flashed across the pirate's face.

"Someone doesn't know as much as he thinks," Grandpa said. He drew a long, thin rope from a belt pouch. Stepping behind the captain, he began to wrap it around the man's waist and arms. The pirate was so shocked by their lack of fear that he let it happen with little fuss.

Archie drew three arrows from his quiver and tied the other end of Grandpa's rope to the shafts. "See, the beast can feed on whole ships, but it doesn't have to," Archie explained. "Not if we give it something else first. Like a snack."

The captain's eyes widened. "No! Wait! Don't be hasty. Let's talk—"

"Words are cheap," said Grandpa. "Actions are gold."

Nocking all three arrows, Archie drew back the string and aimed high. "Enjoy your flight!"

He loosed the arrows. The first one exploded, its force pulling the pirate captain into the air. As he flew ahead of his own ship and over the water, the second and third arrows exploded. On plumes of purple fire, he arced toward the whirlpool and dropped down into the center of the vortex, disappearing under the deep.

A tremor passed through the water. The sea around the whirlpool churned and bubbled. As the ship touched its edge, the whirlpool dissipated just in time for them to sail through safely.

"I love a good twist ending," Archie said.

He and Grandpa shared a laugh, then set about pointing their new ship in the right direction. They had friends to rescue.

They sailed on through the setting sun, and then into the night. Through calm and storms, through fog and starry skies, they raced toward an island that few mortals had found and even fewer had escaped. An island protected from aerial invasion—which was why they had commandeered the ship.

As a red sun rose the next morning, the island appeared on the horizon, beautiful and dangerous.

Closer . . .

The island filled their vision.

Closer . . .

Waves churned on the sparkling shore.

Closer . . .

Grandpa gripped the wheel tightly while Archie grabbed the railing. With a great shudder, the pirate ship rammed into the island and cut halfway up the beach, throwing a tidal wave of wet sand.

When it ground to a stop, they dashed to the prow and peered over the side. Surely the enemy had seen them approach. There would be no surprise attacks. Not against *her*, and—

There she was. Standing in shadow where the trees ended and the beach began, she waited. Beautiful beyond belief, and even more dangerous, it was she who held their friends captive. A monster wrapped in illusion.

Before she could weave her charms, Archie and Grandpa leapt overboard with battle cries. As soon as their feet touched the sand, they drew weapons and charged.

~~~

There were more stars than black in the sky tonight, glittering like gems.

Leaning back on his elbows, Archie gazed up at them in wonder. If he unfocused his eyes, the glow of the island's tiny flame elementals mingled with starlight, and the heavens seemed like they were dancing.

He wore a lazy smile, his heart filled with victory, his belly filled with the meat they had roasted. Grandpa sat across the campfire, savoring his last few bites. Their rescued friends lay around them, sleeping soundly to recover from captivity.

The island was colder at night than Archie had expected. When they found this clearing after vanquishing the monster, they had built the biggest fire they dared to without setting the wilderness ablaze. Even so, he shivered and rubbed his arms.

"I'm chilly too. Almost November, after all," Grandpa said. "We should probably head back soon."

"If we can remember where we parked the ship."

Grandpa chuckled. He nodded at something past Archie.

"Oh, I remember. And when your mother gets back, we'll both be in trouble."

Archie turned to see their riding lawnmower a short distance away. As soon as he saw that reminder of the real world, the shared bubble of fantasy began to fade.

The lawnmower had been their commandeered pirate ship. It sat atop a half-destroyed rosebush, which they had accidentally run over in their fervor to reach the island. Mom guarded those rosebushes with her life. *Oops.*

"Think she'll believe us if we blame pirates?" Archie said.

"Can't hurt to try."

They shared a knowing grin. He was willing to face any consequences Mom gave him, because when he looked at Grandpa now, Archie saw the man he remembered. Once again, weaving story with memory had worked. It had brought him back. If only Archie could solve every problem that way.

With those thoughts, the remainder of the fantasy dissipated like mist. The roaring campfire was back to being their small fire pit. The mythical beast they feasted on became pork chops. The flame elementals were just fireflies.

The night sky remained the same, a blanket of

velvet and diamonds. Archie sighed. At least that part had been real.

"Something on your mind, Fletch?" Grandpa said. "Your soul's lookin' heavy."

Archie shrugged. "The real world, I guess. This project . . . I'm the only one with no clue what I'm going to do. Seems like everyone else has their lives all planned out. But when I think about the future, I just don't know."

Grandpa faced the fire and studied the flames, chewing the inside of his cheek as if deep in thought. For long moments he stared, a troubled expression on his face.

"You're not s'posed to know yet," he finally said. "That should be part of the fun when you're thirteen. But it sounds like you need a better answer than that."

He grimaced. Archie wasn't sure how to describe the expression, but he thought it looked like regret.

"So many things I wanted to tell you," Grandpa continued. "I had all these speeches planned for when you hit certain ages, came to certain moments. First job, first car, first big mistake. First love. All the big things, and some little ones in between. But now time's slippin' away. I can feel it. Won't be long before I can't . . ."

Grandpa shook his head, looking drawn and tired and sad. Then, with effort, he sat up straight and squared his shoulders.

"So I'll just have to tell you some of it early." He locked eyes with Archie. "See, the world at large has it wrong. They focus on what you're going to do, and not on who you're going to be. But what *really* steers the course of your life is the kind of person you are. What you value. What you stand for. That's what'll guide you through life when all you can see is fog—keep you going when you think you can't. And when you break through the fog—when you find purpose and faith and love—it'll help you make the most of them. Once you know who you are, you'll know what to do. And you know what? If you want to, you can choose again. That's another thing they never tell you."

"What do you mean?"

"You get more than one choice in life. You could hit thirty or forty or even fifty and decide you want something new. That's okay. Being an adult is never about having all the answers, because no one ever does. It's about *finding* the answers, and that's a whole lot easier when . . ."

He gestured to Archie.

"When I know who I am," Archie finished.

Smiling, Grandpa nodded. "I know that doesn't help with your project," he said. "But you're already becoming a good man, Fletch. I have faith you'll figure out the rest."

Archie smiled back. "Thanks."

Grandpa nodded and squeezed Archie's shoulder. Then they fell into companionable silence. For the first time in a long time, Archie felt a blanket of peace drape over both of them. A small blanket, but a warm one.

They gazed into the fire as it dwindled to the last glowing embers.

Chapter 9

Only one hour left.

Archie whirled through the kitchen like a Tasmanian devil, a bundle of nervous energy. Everything needed to be perfect, and he hadn't allowed nearly enough time to get it all ready.

He just hadn't been able to put down that Green Arrow comic. And then *Foundation*, one of his old favorites, was just sitting on his desk all alone . . .

It didn't matter now. What mattered were the clock that wouldn't stop ticking and the snacks that he'd been foolish enough to try making. Right now there were two different types of cookies in the oven, and he was busy mixing batters for a third.

Leaning back against the counter, Zig chuckled.

"Dude, you remember this is what I do, right? I can help."

"Aren't you busy with your ramen?"

"You know I can do both."

"Thanks, man, but I need to do it myself."

"Because of Desta?"

Archie paused. "Well . . . girls like a guy who cooks, right?"

"Oh, sure. That's why I have ladies crawling all over me right now." Zig studied the empty air around him. "You see them, too, right?"

Laughing, Archie cracked open the oven to check on his work. Not ready yet.

"You're making dip too?" Zig said. "At least let me do that."

Reluctantly, Archie nodded. "Okay. Thanks."

As Zig went to work, moving with the efficiency of a real chef, Archie refocused on his cookies and the reasons they needed to be perfect.

The last three months had flown by, evaporating before his eyes. Today was the group's first meeting since before winter break, and Archie had foolishly volunteered to host.

The chance to have Desta Senai in his house was worth the anxiety—which he now had tons of.

It wasn't just the food and the ticking clock. Archie still hadn't made a final choice for his project. He'd researched so many options and felt great about them in the moment, but eventually discarded them all. Travel writer, marine biologist, wildlife photographer, airline pilot, seismologist, and astronaut had all been considered and then abandoned. Crime-fighting vigilante might also have been on the table for a brief moment, but that required either superpowers or a ton of inherited money.

He was still keeping "novelist" in his back pocket. If all else failed, it was the choice that made the most sense. But which choice came from his heart? He wished he knew.

What would Desta think when she found out he still couldn't decide? She was probably halfway finished with her project by now.

He hoped tonight would give him one-on-one time with her, a chance to talk about more than just the project and get a better read on her. All Desta's interactions with him were friendly, but she treated everyone that way. Archie had seen how a girl looked at a guy when she wanted to be more than friends. Desta had never looked at him that way. A couple of times he had built up the courage to drop subtle hints about his interest, but if she picked up on them, she didn't show it.

So maybe fresh cookies were the way to her heart. Probably not, but it wasn't like he had better ideas.

"Mmm, those smell great, Zig." Mom bustled into the kitchen, looking just as anxious as Archie. Maybe more.

She wore a new dress. Archie had seen new matching shoes waiting in a box too. Her brown hair was still flying loose and unstyled, though, and she must have left the mirror halfway through applying makeup.

"Don't look at me." Zig grinned, pointing at Archie.

Mom's eyebrows shot up. "Really? Wow."

"Maybe save that wow until they're finished and not burned," Archie said.

"I have faith in you," she replied. "You shouldn't have to worry about your grandfather tonight. He had a good morning, and he's reading in his room now."

"You're going soon?"

"About half an hour. Blane's picking me up."

Blane? Archie hadn't met this one either. He moved past it before the thought could show on his face. "Okay," he said. "We'll be fine."

As if on cue, Grandpa appeared at the doorway,

holding a decades-old Justice Society comic book with his thumb marking his place. He stopped at the kitchen and swiveled his head to take in the surroundings. When his eyes settled on Archie, they took a moment too long to show recognition.

Grandpa nodded at him. "Grandson." He did the same with Mom. "Daughter."

Like he was reminding himself how to label them but couldn't remember their actual names. He peered at the room itself.

"Kitchen. This is my house."

Archie exchanged a tense look with Mom.

This wasn't a bad day. They had seen those before. Days when Grandpa remembered just enough to know he was forgetting, and the frustration boiled over into bursts of rage unlike any Archie had ever seen from Grandpa.

But it wasn't a good day, when he could easily look after himself. And he often got more disoriented in the evenings.

Please, not now, Archie pleaded with the universe. *Why now?*

Mom visibly collected herself. When she spoke, her voice was gentle. "Yes, Dad, this is your house. Do you need anything?"

Grandpa shook his head, then walked past her to stand at the window. With narrowed eyes he studied the backyard. "Grass needs mowing."

"It's winter," Archie said.

"Where's the riding mower?"

"It's *winter*," Archie said more forcefully.

Mom gave him a look. He made himself take a breath. Snapping at Grandpa wouldn't help, but sometimes Archie just couldn't hold in his frustration. From the corner of his eye, he saw Zig back out of the kitchen.

"I'll take care of it," Grandpa said, as if Archie hadn't responded.

He moved toward the back door, and Archie's anxiety skyrocketed. The mower was in the utility shed. Under no circumstances could they let him onto that machine.

If they didn't distract him enough, a frustrating situation could become a scary one. But if they distracted him in the wrong way, that could go badly too.

Archie floated in indecision. Someone needed to handle Grandpa, but the study group was less than an hour away. He turned to Mom and saw the same dilemma on her face. Her date, whoever he was, couldn't be far away.

Mom's expression turned plaintive. "Archie . . ."

He knew what she wanted before she said it. "I can't! My group's coming, and you know that usually takes a while to work."

"I know this isn't fair, but we're desperate."

The shared fantasies. After months of success, Mom had seen firsthand how effective they could be in bringing Grandpa back. She wasn't convinced that they could be a long-term solution, but she couldn't deny that they'd worked well so far. The potent combination of adventure stories and old memories spoke to the core of Raymond Reese.

"I don't have anything ready!" Archie said. "I've used up all the best stories."

It sounded like a feeble excuse, but it was true. Archie and Grandpa had been superheroes flying through a collapsing building to save helpless citizens. Then space explorers defending the galaxy from hostile aliens. Then scientists searching for a way to keep the sun from exploding.

And more, and more, and more.

Archie was reading books at a faster pace than ever. He had practically memorized the Journal stories he was allowed to read. He had fallen behind on homework and chores.

Because recycling stories rarely turned out well. The spark was gone; Grandpa wouldn't engage the same way he had the first time. But coming up with new scenarios—both real and imagined—did work. Archie had never forgotten what the doctor said. *No known cure.* But what if Grandpa didn't need a cure? What if Archie could help keep the disease at bay, prevent it from progressing any further?

There was no reason to think he couldn't keep this up for a long time. Who knew—maybe one day someone would write a scholarly paper about the radical new therapy Archie had discovered.

But hopes for the future didn't relieve any of the tension right now. In this moment, Archie had nothing.

"Archie, please," Mom said.

"This is the worst."

"I know. I'm sorry."

Zig reappeared at Archie's side and spoke softly. "Don't worry, I can finish in here. Go look after him. We'll be ready."

A trickle of relief flowed through Archie. He gave his best friend a grateful look, then turned back to Mom.

"Okay. I'll try."

~~~

Grandpa had been holding a Justice Society comic—an old one from an era long past. It was all the inspiration Archie had to work with, and he had only minutes to come up with a functional fantasy world.

This one didn't fold in any stories from the Journal, so he just did what he could to make it interesting. Starting with their wardrobe: dapper suits and fedoras, with black masks covering the top halves of their faces. Very retro.

Running at top speed, Archie kicked off the wall and flipped behind the enemy that had been chasing him—an assassin in black robes and a mask. With a flash, Archie's baton struck home and the assassin burst into smoke.

Something moved behind him. Dropping to the ground, he rolled away as a hailstorm of throwing knives filled the air where he'd been. The roll took him past Grandpa before he leapt to his feet and stood so they were back to back.

"They're coming from all sides," he warned.

". . . right," Grandpa said. "Okay."

Archie couldn't worry about the tension in

Grandpa's voice. Their mission had been discovered right on the verge of success, and the enemy had sent their deadliest force to stop the two masked vigilantes from escaping with the intel. The small office they had tried to hide in was now their battleground as assassins came at them from all directions.

He pointed over Grandpa's shoulder. "More coming that way. Be ready."

Two knives flew at him from the shadows. He couldn't bring up his baton quickly enough, and dodging would just let them hit Grandpa in the back. Gritting his teeth, Archie dropped the baton and threw up his hands.

And somehow managed to catch both knives. With a whoop of triumph, Archie hurled them back the way they had come. Twin *thunk*s, and another assassin turned to smoke.

Grandpa's two enemies had been joined by three more, and all five were coming for him. But he just stood there.

Archie spun to face them and tried to swing his baton—the baton he had just dropped. *Great.*

Reaching under his jacket, he palmed a small device, which unfolded to reveal a tiny auto crossbow. He aimed and pulled the trigger. Two assassins puffed away, then a third, their masks dropping to the floor.

The fourth assassin struck at Grandpa with a blade. No time to think. Archie dropped his weapon and grabbed the blade. The cold steel bit into his hands as he halted it mere inches from Grandpa's heart.

Now was the moment. Archie had the enemy just where he wanted. He gripped the blade tightly, keeping the assassin from drawing it back, and cast an expectant look at Grandpa.

"Do it!"

Grandpa's brow furrowed. When he spoke, it came out as a growl. "Do *what*?"

It wasn't working. None of it was working! Grandpa wasn't coming back, and now his anger was starting to resurface. Panic flashed through Archie just as he heard footsteps. The fifth assassin.

Groaning with pain and exertion, Archie forced the fourth assassin's blade around to meet the threat.

Too slow. The fifth assassin's blade pierced his side.

A sharp burst of agony. An odd sensation of cold.

Archie dropped hard onto his back. He looked up at his grandfather, feeling betrayed but not knowing why. What was happening?

The last two assassins lunged at Grandpa. The instant they touched him, they burst into smoke. Then the office did the same, along with all their suits and masks.

Just like that, the fantasy fractured.

Chapter 10

Rain poured as if the sky had unzipped to empty the clouds all at once. Lightning lit the gloom. Archie flinched at a crack of thunder.

He pulled the last cookie sheet out of the oven and started transferring cookies to the cooling rack. The enticing aroma didn't touch his senses, and the warmth didn't soothe his nerves.

His mind floated in a storm cloud too. It rained frustration and fear. Like bolts of lightning, a question bounced through his thoughts over and over again.

Why did I fail?

His efforts hadn't been a total bust. During their fantasy, Archie had been able to redirect Grandpa into the garage and away from the utility shed. By the time it fell to pieces, Grandpa had forgotten about mowing the lawn.

But the real Raymond Reese hadn't come back. He was still lost inside Grandpa's head, contending with an enemy that grew stronger by the day. Alzheimer's was a real jerk.

Archie had theories but no way to know if they were right. The fantasy hadn't included details from the Journal, and he hadn't had time to craft a good story. He had also tried it when Grandpa had already fully lost touch with himself and his surroundings, while before he'd been able to catch him at the beginning of the downward slide.

Then there was the hero element. Grandpa had spent so many years protecting people. With this fantasy, though, they were only defending themselves. No clear goals, evil plots to foil, or people to help.

Then the rage had returned. Just a short burst, and Grandpa had managed to regain control quickly. The doctors had warned them it would happen more often. As Grandpa's mind deteriorated, he'd have to grapple with the frustration of not being able to remember things, the infuriating tip-of-your-tongue feeling of knowing something was missing but not being able to pinpoint what.

And as good memories faded, they left more

room for bad ones to resurface. Grandpa still wouldn't talk about them, but sometimes Archie could see them eating away at him from the inside. What could have happened in Grandpa's past that was so bad?

Any of these could be the reason the fantasy had failed. Or all of them. Or none of them.

Archie clenched his jaw, desperate determination welling up inside. He would throw himself deeper into stories. He would memorize every line of that Journal. He would hold back the disease like a dam, keeping Grandpa as the man he knew for as long as possible.

The doorbell rang. Archie's heart leapt into his throat. Was Desta here early?

He approached the front door, working to breathe steadily. Shoulders back, he plastered on a smile and opened the door.

His face fell. "Oh, hey. What are you doing here?"

"Great to see you too," Uncle Dan said. "Would you feel better if I said I brought pizza?"

Archie looked at his uncle's hands. Except for an umbrella, they were empty.

"Did you?"

"No, but that would've been awesome, right?"

Archie laughed. Uncle Dan had that effect on people.

A throat cleared, and Aunt Candace peeked around from behind her husband. "Daniel, it's raining."

"Yes, my love." Uncle Dan glanced up at the umbrella sheltering them both. "If only humanity had invented a device to deal with that kind of thing."

Aunt Candace rolled her eyes, but Archie caught a hint of a smile. "Archibald, let us in," she said.

As they stepped inside, Aunt Candace turned and looked back at the driveway. Instantly her expression turned stern again.

"What are you doing?" she demanded. "Get in here."

"I'm communing with nature!" Aunt Violet said.

Standing without an umbrella, she held her arms out wide, her face tilted up toward the storm.

"If you commune with lightning, that'll be a quick conversation," Uncle Dan said.

"You city types never understand," Aunt Violet chided. "All you know is your offices and your lattes and your—"

A crack of thunder shook the air. Aunt Violet yelped and sprinted toward the house. When she made it inside, they were all struggling not to laugh.

"Whew!" Aunt Violet shook herself like a wet dog. "She's in a bad mood today."

"She?" Archie asked.

"Nature, silly," she replied, ruffling his hair.

"You didn't even need to come," Aunt Candace said.

Aunt Violet frowned. "Penny asked for my help."

"That was a group text. She asked for *anyone's* help, and we said we would come."

"And so did I." Aunt Violet raised her chin in defiance. "You just don't think I can take care of Dad, but I'm the one who taught him how to do *this*."

Arms raised, she shimmied rhythmically in a dance that Archie didn't recognize.

Aunt Candace bristled. "Do you even know how ridic—"

She stopped as Uncle Dan squeezed her shoulder. With a glance at him, she seemed to decompress. When Uncle Dan lowered his hand, she reached out to hold it and almost smiled.

Wow, Archie thought, *she's capable of human emotion after all.*

But he was still confused. "Mom didn't say anyone was coming. Why—?"

"Yo."

The family turned toward the open door. They had forgotten to close it. Now someone new leaned against the doorway like he was the coolest dude in the bar.

"Um, can I help you?" Archie said.

"I don't know, junior. Can you?" The guy laughed. When no one else did, he pursed his lips and stepped inside. "Name's Blane. I'm sure Penny's talked about me."

Archie eyed him head to toe. Frost-tipped hair spiked up with gel. Tinted nonprescription glasses. Button-up shirt with way too many buttons undone. Too-tight jeans that flared at the bottom to reveal fake snakeskin boots, and a fake snakeskin jacket to match. And he hadn't bothered to use an umbrella, so all of it was damp.

Archie stared at this ludicrous man, agape. Was Mom kidding?

Uncle Dan snapped his fingers in recognition. "You're the mechanic from that import shop, right?"

Blane's arrogance dropped a notch. "No."

"Oh. The shoe salesman?"

"No."

"French teacher at the community college?"

Blane's jaw clenched. "No, man."

"Hmm." Uncle Dan tapped his chin, appearing confused. "I don't get it, Dane. You must have come up at some point, or . . ."

"It's Blane," he said through gritted teeth.

"Oh. Then no, she hasn't talked about you."

Uncle Dan kept a mostly straight face, but his eyes twinkled. All Blane could do was stand there and fume while someone pretended not to make fun of him.

Archie wished he could have laughed, but this was the last straw. His own jaw clenched now. "Just hold on, *Blane*," he said coldly. "I'll tell her you're here."

Archie stomped upstairs and stopped squarely in Mom's doorway. She was at her vanity, applying finishing touches to her makeup.

"Really?" he said. "That guy?"

"What do you mean?"

"I mean the most ridiculous human in the world is waiting for you. What are you doing?"

Mom was still looking in the mirror, but he saw her go cold. "You're too young to understand, and who I date is not your business."

If Archie were a cartoon, steam would have jetted from his ears. "You know that's a lie. For months, you haven't explained why you're dating every guy in Missouri, and I haven't asked. But this isn't like you anymore."

Archie knew his emotions were running away with him. Now that the bottle was uncorked, frustrations he'd buried were spilling over and he couldn't stop himself.

"You talk about working together, but you don't actually do it. Now you're running off with guys like him. And you called in babysitters when you know I'm too old for—"

"Babysitters?"

"Your sisters and Uncle Dan. Do you want my classmates to think I'm too much of a kid to take care of myself? I mean . . ."

The ice in Mom's expression melted. In a blink, she changed from defensive to struggling not to cry. It was only then that Archie understood.

"Oh," he said. "They . . . they aren't here for me, are they?"

Mom shook her head. "They're going to take your grandpa out to get dinner, then stay here with him until I get home." Her chin started to quiver.

Now Archie was holding back his own tears. He had known this would happen someday, but now that someday was *today*, it felt like a tidal wave had crashed down on him.

The time had come when Grandpa—the toughest man he'd ever known—couldn't look after himself for an evening. That was why Mom had texted their family at the last minute.

But why hadn't she just canceled her date? Why was going out with *Blane* more important than anything else? He knew he should apologize, but the war of emotions collected in his throat and choked off the words. So, feeling like the jerk of the century, he turned and left Mom there alone.

Taking refuge in his room, he closed the door and sat on his bed, staring at nothing. A few minutes later he heard Mom leave with Blane.

For too long he just sat there, knowing the clock was counting down. Knowing Desta was coming and he would have to try to be charming. But wanting nothing more than to bury his head under a pillow and wish the world away.

Chapter 11

Archie stood at the closed front door like he was about to face a firing squad. He had heard a car coming up the driveway, and now he could see it through the stained glass pane in the door.

The moment had arrived. He wished he could feel happier about it.

Zig bumped his shoulder. "Hey, man. I don't know what happened, and I won't ask, but you've got this. I'll back you up all the way."

Archie gave a wan smile. "Thanks, Zig. I need it."

Only Spencer's car had arrived, but Desta and Kamiko were climbing out with him. Desta had ridden here with Spencer. Archie felt a pang of jealousy, then felt foolish for feeling jealous. He tried to bury it and focus on enjoying himself.

A knock on the door. With one quick, deep

breath, Archie put on a casual smile and opened it. "Hey, come on in."

"Hey yourself," Desta said, her smile sending a zing up Archie's spine. Stepping inside, she handed him a grocery bag. "I brought some cookies, but— hey, it smells great in here."

"Archie made cookies," Zig said.

Her eyebrows rose. "Really? Wow. Then you definitely won't want these."

"No, I'm sure they're great," Archie said. "Thanks."

Kamiko came through the door next, carrying drinks. "What up, Arch? Hey, Zig. Tell me you made something awesome."

"Ramen's cooking now. Archie made the cookies, though."

"Right on," Kamiko said.

Spencer stepped inside last, and Archie had to work not to roll his eyes. How many sizes too small was that T-shirt? Spencer seemed to be flexing with every motion. No doubt he'd be working for Desta's attention all evening.

Archie glanced down at his own clothes—baggy to hide the extra pounds he carried. If he had Spencer's toned stomach, would he want to show it off too? He buried the thought before it could drain his small supply of confidence.

Spencer handed over a bag with chips and salsa. Instead of looking at Archie, he studied the living room as if evaluating a piece of livestock.

"So, this is where you live, huh?" he said. The words were innocent, but the tone wasn't.

"Hey, come on," Desta said. "It's a great house, Archie."

Zig looked at Spencer. "Didn't your family make its money with sewage treatment?" Spencer's face turned red. Before he could come up with a retort, Zig turned away. "Anyway, who's hungry?"

Zig led everyone through the kitchen and into the dining room, which didn't get much use these days but had a bigger table than the kitchen. To Archie's surprise, Spencer held back. When he looked at Archie now, he almost seemed embarrassed.

"Hey, uh, thanks for having us," he said. "Or whatever."

Saying that probably felt like ripping off an arm. Archie nodded and tried to accept it. Resenting Spencer all day wouldn't help anything, so he decided to let it go.

Archie paused in the kitchen to get the snacks and drinks organized. Desta stayed with him.

"How can I help?" she asked.

"Oh. Um," he stammered. "Maybe put the cookies on that tray? I'll get bowls ready for Zig's ramen. Then maybe we can both get drinks."

"Sure."

They went to work, falling into a shared quiet that felt oddly comfortable. Archie could hear their friends' chatter from the dining room but couldn't have repeated anything they said. All his thoughts and senses were trained on Desta. On enjoying her closeness.

Still, his insides screamed at him to come up with something to talk about. To fill the quiet and create some magical moment. To do something that would help Desta really see him.

The soup was ready. He reached for a glass . . .

. . . and froze as his hand wrapped around Desta's.

She had reached for the same glass. Now she stood frozen too. He could see the surprise in her eyes.

Sparks raced up Archie's arm. Starting at the point where they touched and ending at his chest, they leapt and crackled and burst under his skin like tiny fireworks. His mind raced while feeling like it was floating in molasses at the same time. Was this really happening? Was her surprise more like *yes thank you finally* or *ew don't touch me*?

It lasted maybe a second and a half, but it felt like forever. Then Archie finally had a clear thought. *LET GO.*

They pulled back at the same time. Archie tried to look casual while suppressing a nervous giggle and clearing his throat all at once. Desta stared at the counter and brushed her hair behind her ears.

Just as Archie worked up the nerve to look her in the eye, she did the same. They shared a quick glance and a sheepish grin. Desta recovered faster than Archie. Squaring her shoulders, she reached for a different glass and filled it with ice.

"So, um, you grew up in this house?" she said.

Archie stared for another second before remembering to respond. He flinched and grabbed a glass. "Uh, yeah. My grandfather built it."

"I feel like we've lost that," Desta said. "Our generation, I mean. You know? Like, do any of us actually know how to build anything?"

"We're pretty good with internet memes," Archie joked. "But you're right. Maybe I should ask Grandpa to teach me some of those skills before . . ."

The second half of that thought hit him like a freight train out of a foggy night. Mentally he finished the sentence his lips couldn't say.

. . . *before he can't anymore.*

He looked up to find Desta gazing at him with concern.

She lowered her voice. "I've heard about what's happening. How is he?"

Archie wanted to act like he was fine, but his tough mask couldn't hold up under the kindness in her voice. He sighed. "It's like watching someone you love sink into quicksand. The worst part is that he feels it happening. Some days I can help, but others, I just have to watch him sink."

"I'm sorry," Desta said. "Can we do anything?"

Archie gave her a grateful look. "Having everyone here is nice, especially today when other stuff feels . . . wrong."

"What do you mean?" Desta held up a hand. "Wait, sorry, that's none of my business."

"No, it's okay. I mean, um . . ." Archie hesitated. Only Zig knew about this. Then he reminded himself who he was talking to. "My mom's been single my whole life, so I'm used to her dating. But lately, it feels like she's been going on dates practically every night, with a different guy each time, and they're getting less and less likable. It's like she ran out of good ones, so now she's finding all the leftover jerks. And she picks *now* to start this, when we already have so much to worry about."

He stopped before words could keep pouring out and embarrass him even more. Instead he grabbed another glass. "Anyway, I just don't get it."

The silence stretched until his glass was full. When he reached for the next one, Desta spoke.

"Can I ask you something?"

"Sure."

"You've both lived with your grandfather this whole time?"

"Yeah. And my grandmother, before she passed away."

"Your dad was never around?"

"Divorced before I was born."

Desta started to speak, then hesitated.

"It's okay," Archie said. "Say it."

"Well," Desta said slowly, "look, I don't know your family, but when my dad's father died, I saw what grief can do to people. It's not pretty. Or, maybe it's not really about the grief. Maybe it's . . ."

Brow furrowed, she bit her bottom lip. He knew

he should be focusing on the conversation, but wow, that lip bite.

"More about family?" Desta finished. "Like, your mom had a family, but now that your grandfather is sick, could she be . . . I don't know, trying to fill the void?"

Archie rocked back. He hadn't considered that. Desta had held up a mirror, and suddenly Archie saw how selfish he'd been. Because he wasn't the only one losing someone he loved.

"Archie, I'm sorry," Desta said. "That was probably out of line."

"No, you're right. I never thought how this might hurt differently for Mom." His face twisted with regret. "And I threw it in her face today."

"I'm sure she knows you love her."

Archie nodded. If Desta was right, then things needed to change with Mom. They had to work harder to understand each other. Otherwise they'd just keep hurting each other when they needed support the most.

"Thanks," he said. "That helps."

Footsteps interrupted the moment. Archie's aunts and uncle appeared at the kitchen door.

"Party time, Archie?" Uncle Dan asked.

"A nerdy one, I guess. We're doing a project." Archie saw Uncle Dan's eyes flick toward Desta. "Oh, right. Desta, this is Uncle Dan and my aunts, Candace and Violet."

As they all exchanged greetings, Grandpa shuffled into the kitchen. His eyes were just as foggy as they'd been earlier, but Archie couldn't resist the urge to make one more introduction.

"Grandpa, this is Desta Senai," he said. "Desta, Raymond Reese."

Desta held out her hand. "A pleasure, sir."

Grandpa grasped her hand with the grace and style of an old country gentleman. "Pleasure's all mine, miss." Then he squinted, as if he were trying to figure something out. "You're on my grandson's phone."

"Okaaaay," Archie said, herding his family toward the door. "Thanks Grandpa and everyone for saying hi now have a great dinner goodbye!"

When the front door closed, he turned back to Desta, knowing that his face was beet red. "He, um, probably thinks you're Siri. You know old people and phones."

"Oh, of course." She nodded graciously and picked up the tray of cookies. "Shall we?"

Hoping that he wasn't blushing, Archie followed her into the dining room with drinks in hand.

~~~

"So," Desta began. "How's everyone's project going, and who needs help? You want to start, Spencer?"

"Nah, I'm cool." Spencer leaned back in his chair. "I made a list of big charities that are run by boards, so now I just gotta pick a couple. Then I can grab stuff from their websites and talk about what they do in the essay. Home run."

"What kind of charities are you focusing on?" Desta asked.

"I'm thinking something to do with the environment."

"That's still pretty broad," Archie pointed out.

Spencer shrugged. "I mean, a good cause is a good cause, right?"

Archie suppressed a sigh. Did Spencer even realize what a rich kid stereotype he was? Probably not. Self-awareness didn't seem to be one of his priorities.

"I've narrowed down to two ramen recipes," Zig said. "You're eating the first one. The second is a more radical idea. I'll make that for you next time."

"Dude, if it's half as amazing as this one, it'll be a winner." Kamiko sipped another spoonful and shivered. "This tastes so good, it's scary."

Zig beamed. "Thanks. But picking the recipe is the easy part. I've got to plan this like I'm opening a pop-up restaurant. That means getting permits to cook at the exhibit hall, figuring out how to refrigerate my ingredients, and estimating how many people I need to feed."

"Will you need a special permit to use open flames?" Archie asked.

"Got that figured out, actually. If I use induction burners, I can cook superfast and I don't have to worry about fire."

"Wow, that's ambitious," Desta said. "I like it. How can we help?"

Zig flashed an embarrassed smile. "Well, I sat down to write the essay, and the only thing I came up with was a menu and one paragraph about how dark the world would be without flavor. So, any ideas?"

"Heritage!" Archie blurted.

He winced when all eyes turned on him. The idea had just popped out of his mouth.

"I like saying random words too," said Spencer. "Bananas! Pogo stick! Giant nerd!"

144

"What I mean is . . ." Archie took a breath to gather himself, and to bury his annoyance at Spencer. "*Your* heritage, Zig. Don't chefs talk about food that way? Especially chefs who do fusion of some kind. Like it's a way to share their cultures and traditions? Maybe you could write about that."

Zig tapped his chin, pondering, and his look of concentration became a broad grin. It was like watching a light bulb slowly get brighter. "Sharing traditions . . . mixing the old with the new . . . putting a fresh spin on family legacies . . . Yeah, I like that. Thanks, bro, I'll give it a shot."

"Kam," Desta said. "You haven't told us what you're doing next."

Kamiko grimaced. "Yeah, about that. I don't think it's going to work."

"Are you sure? It was a great idea," Zig said.

"I was really stoked, but no animal shelters are taking me seriously. I've volunteered before, and I've tried explaining about the project, but the volunteer coordinators keep saying I'm too young for them to work with. If I can't get them to trust me with any of their animals for the night of the gala, how am I supposed to do this?"

"Wait, you were serious about that?" Spencer

said. "Like, taking care of the animals yourself? I figured you just wanted to own an animal hospital or something."

Kamiko looked askance at him. "No, dude, I want to get in there and do the actual work. That's the whole point of becoming a vet."

"Oh." Spencer looked down at the table, his brow furrowed. "Yeah, um, I guess that makes sense."

Weird. But Archie didn't spend any time focusing on Spencer. "Hey, Kam, what's your essay going to say?" he asked.

"I'm not even close to knowing that," she replied. "I mean, no one will even work with me, so how am I supposed to start writing about it? I may just have to pick a whole new project."

"Well, I might have an idea," said Archie. "But it's kind of out there."

She leaned forward. "I'll take 'out there.' Whatcha got?"

"What if you wrote from the point of view of a rescue animal? It starts out lonely and afraid, and then you show the moment when a family comes to adopt it, so it goes from hopeless to happy. You can explain the process of how pets get adopted, and you can ask someone at the shelter to read it for accuracy. Then maybe they'll see how serious you are."

"Huh." Kamiko leaned back in her chair. "You know, Arch, that could work. And if they don't go for it, at least I'll still have a good essay."

Archie grinned, then turned to Desta. "How about you? Need any help?"

She gave him a smile that set his heart racing. "Anyone want to let me operate on them at the event?"

The group laughed while Desta threw up her hands in mock exasperation.

"No one's willing to go the extra mile? I see how it is. Guess I'll find some other way to make this project interesting."

"You could start by choosing what kind of surgeon you want to be," Kamiko offered. "Aren't there different, like, specialties or something?"

Desta nodded slowly, gently biting her bottom lip as she considered Kamiko's suggestion. Archie worked hard not to stare at her lips.

"Yeah," Desta said. "I've been putting that off, but I guess you're right, Kam. That'll be my next step."

To Archie, she seemed more resigned than excited. If this was really the career she wanted, wouldn't she be enjoying her project more?

The next hour flew by. Spencer stayed uncharacteristically quiet, as if he had something on his mind, but everyone else relaxed into a rhythm, trading ideas and making plans.

At some point, Archie heard his family return from dinner. A little later, Aunt Candace and Uncle Dan said goodbye on their way out. Aunt Violet was staying behind to watch Grandpa until Mom got home. After that, the house beyond the dining room was quiet, so Archie let himself keep concentrating on his guests.

Eventually, the discussion drifted toward other topics. Movies that had come out recently. The only new restaurant that had opened in their little town. Things that friends talked about. The evening had turned out way better than it had started.

It felt good just to be a kid, even for a short while.

Chapter 12

Two cars idled in the driveway, waiting to take everyone home. Holding the front door open, Archie said goodbye to his study partners as they filed out. Zig headed toward one car, Kamiko and Spencer toward the other. Desta stepped outside last, then turned back.

"This was really nice," she said. "Your cookies were great."

"Oh." Archie glanced down and rubbed the back of his neck, caught off guard by the compliment. "Yeah, no problem. Glad you could come."

"And I know you'll find a project. When you do, we'll be there to help, just like you've helped us." She gave him a feather-light punch in the shoulder. "We've got your back."

Sparks danced under his skin again where she'd

touched him. He tried to respond, but his brain had forgotten how to use words. Instead he offered what he hoped was a grateful smile.

With a little wave, Desta turned and walked toward Spencer's car. Archie watched after her, secretly hoping she would look back at him. But she didn't, and they sped away.

He shut the front door, trying to dispel his disappointment. It had been a good day, even if she treated him like just a friend. Not that being friends was bad. Being friends was nice.

Though it would've been nicer if she'd looked back.

As Archie walked through the living room, Aunt Violet snored, sprawled facedown on the couch.

Yeah, that seems about right.

With a snort, she sat bolt upright. "What? I'm awake, I swear!" When her bleary eyes landed on Archie, her expression turned mortified. "Don't tell Candace."

"Your secret's safe with me," Archie said with mock drama.

No harm done, he figured. Grandpa needed an adult around in case he got confused or upset, but he didn't need someone tracking his every movement—even if Aunt Candace might think so.

Leaving Violet to gather herself, he ambled toward the kitchen. He hadn't eaten much while the group was here. Stress made him ravenous, but he'd felt too self-conscious to wolf down a big bowl of food in front of everyone. Now he could snack without an audience, and Zig's leftover ramen was calling his name.

In the kitchen doorway, Archie stopped in his tracks. Grandpa was standing at the refrigerator.

"Oh hey, Grandpa. I thought you went to bed."

Grandpa didn't respond. Head buried in the fridge, he rifled through its contents with urgency, as if he'd lost something in there.

"Looking for something?" Archie asked. "There's peanut M&Ms in the freezer."

With a shake of his head and a frustrated huff, Grandpa slammed the fridge door shut and shuffled over to the pantry. He threw both doors open and dove into the shelves. Boxes and bags of food rustled loudly as he shoved them around.

What was he looking for? Gingerly, Archie laid a hand on Grandpa's arm. "Can I help you find something?"

Grandpa yanked his arm away. Archie flinched. *It's a bad one.*

Slamming the pantry doors shut, Grandpa glared at Archie. His eyes weren't just cloudy and confused. There was a frenzy behind them, and he stared as if he suspected Archie was an enemy.

"Whoever you are," he seethed, "when I find what I'm looking for, I'll know what it is. Okay? Just leave me alone!"

Grandpa shouldered past him, turned one way and then another, and finally went back to the fridge. Throwing the door open, he searched desperately where he'd already searched before.

All Archie could do was stand there, feeling a sadness that seemed too infinite for one person to contain. Like a chasm that he could never cry enough tears to fill up.

If he believed crying would help, he might have tried. Instead he just felt exhausted, as if that chasm had a physical weight that he'd been carrying all these months.

Flying with dragons together wouldn't fix this. Not tonight.

Aunt Violet was in the other room. If Grandpa got out of control, it was her job to handle him tonight.

But it seemed to Archie that, in moments like this, there was nothing to do except leave Grandpa alone. He would work through his confusion eventually. Hopefully.

Archie sighed. "Good night, Grandpa."

He turned and left the kitchen. Every movement felt like his limbs were filled with concrete. His one comforting thought was that at least Grandma Ella didn't have to see this.

Somehow, he made it up the stairs. He meant to go straight to bed but found himself hovering in the doorway to Grandpa's room. His gaze fixed on a recent painting: mist rolling over rich green hills, a blue sea beyond, and the ruins of an ancient castle perched atop a cliff.

Grandpa sometimes painted memories from his old adventures. This one must be from when he'd traveled across Ireland with nothing but a backpack.

Archie had determined long ago that he would make that same trip someday. He would have to ask Grandpa for more details when he was ready to plan it.

With that thought, reality came flooding back. Archie's heart sank. By the time he was old enough to travel on his own, would he still be able to ask Grandpa about Ireland? Would Grandpa even remember going there?

Feeling twice as heavy now, Archie shuffled into his own bedroom and collapsed onto the bed. He pulled his computer onto his lap. There was still a project to think about, and it had become obvious that life wouldn't wait for him to stop feeling sad.

So he sat there and he searched his own heart, and he pondered.

Who was he? What did he want to be?

How about anywhere but here?

He grimaced, feeling guilty for thinking that. It wasn't true. But right now it felt true. How could he decide his purpose in life when life was cracking apart under his feet?

Footsteps passed by his door—Grandpa going to bed, Aunt Violet checking on him.

He stared at his desk, where the Journal waited beside a new novel Mom had let him buy. This one was about people hopping between dimensions. Could he use that in the next fantasy for Grandpa?

There could be no more winging it. Archie had to be better prepared for the next time Grandpa needed him, or the disease would start winning. He had to focus on that.

But . . .

Even if the Stone-Katzman Project wasn't as world-changing as he'd once believed, shouldn't he keep working until he found a way to finish it? Wasn't thinking about the future an early step in making the future happen?

Still the Journal called to him and the novel sang his name, promising answers. Promising salvation. He reached toward them.

The project will still be there tomorrow.

Didn't you say that last night, and the night before?

Pushing through his own objections, Archie pulled the books onto the bed. Just as he opened the novel to the title page, he heard the front door open. He paused, struck with cold anxiety.

Mom was home.

~~~

Archie waited until he heard Aunt Violet leave and Mom come upstairs before he left his room. Grandpa's door was closed. Archie saw no light along the cracks as he crept by.

At the end of the hall, soft light spilled from Mom's open door. It felt ten miles away. He tried to avoid all the creaky parts of the floor, but his heartbeat pounded so loudly that it was hard to tell if he was successful. Anxiety or not, though, this needed to be done.

After an eternal march, he stopped in her doorway. Mom sat at her vanity, slowly taking down her hair and removing her earrings. No, not slowly. Wearily. Mechanically. She stared into space like her mind was far away.

Archie cleared his throat. Mom went stiff. Her eyes focused but stayed on the mirror.

"How was your date?"

Mom shrugged. "It was . . . well, you know, it was . . ." She sighed, her posture sagging. "Awful. I don't know what I was thinking."

Leaning over, she slipped her shoes off and set them aside. Then she removed her necklace. Though she seemed focused on those simple tasks, Archie could see that her attention was split. She didn't look at him, but she was aware he was still there.

The tension hung thick between them, like something he could physically cut through. He pushed past it. It didn't change what he needed to do.

"I'm sorry," he said. "I never thought how it might affect you, watching Grandpa . . . change."

Trembling, Mom braced both hands on the vanity and took a series of deliberate breaths. Archie wouldn't have known what that meant a year ago. Now he knew she was struggling to hold herself together. Eventually, though, she started to cry.

Archie sat on the bench next to her. She latched onto him, holding tightly. He did the same. Then he realized he was crying too.

He didn't know how long they sat there clinging to each other like they were the only two people in a lifeboat tossed by stormy seas. He just knew that, right now, holding on felt like the only way to survive.

"I never knew how lonely this would feel," Mom said. "And we've both been trying to cope by ourselves."

"But we don't have to."

Mom shook her head. "No. We have to talk more, and we have to be better at facing what's happening—not just trying to distract ourselves from it."

They leaned out of the embrace. Archie took a moment to wipe his eyes.

"I'm so afraid of losing him," Mom confessed. "I've been using all these dates like you use your fantasies with Grandpa. They're an escape, but in the end that's all they are. They won't really change anything. So we need to do better, find ways to deal with all of this for real. We *can* do better, right?"

Archie didn't hear the question. She shook him gently.

"Earth to Archibald."

"What?"

"I said we can help each other do better, right?"

"Oh. Um, yeah. Definitely."

"Good," Mom said.

He tried to look upbeat for Mom's sake. He knew he'd done the right thing, apologizing. Grandpa always said it was what strong people did. And this talk had clearly done Mom so much good. She would feel terrible if she knew how deeply her words had cut him.

The shared fantasies were just an escape? Everything he'd done to protect Grandpa's mind, to hold off the disease—was she saying it didn't really work? That couldn't be true, right? After all, she was the one who'd asked him to use the fantasies today.

And look how that turned out.

They hugged again and said good night. When Archie closed his door and sank into bed, he hoped sleep would overtake him quickly.

But her words wouldn't leave him. Was she right?

Am I doing this the wrong way?

Chapter 13

"Morning, sunshine," Mom said with a smirk.

Coming upstairs, she stopped at the landing as Archie stepped out of his room. He rubbed sleep from his eyes.

"It's too early for a witty comeback," he said.

"Guess that means I win."

Chuckling, Archie slung his backpack over one shoulder. Mom glanced at the book in his other hand and brightened.

"Anything useful?"

"Yeah, I'm taking notes. I might scan some pages too, to share with the family."

"Good!"

It had been a week since Archie and Mom had agreed to be better at helping each other. Their relationship had already started to improve, and the new book was Archie's first attempt to make good on his side of the bargain.

This one wasn't a novel—it was a resource book about Alzheimer's, written specifically for family members caring for someone with the illness. The language was dry as overcooked turkey, and Archie had to fight to keep his eyes from crossing every time he read it, but the information was useful.

The book recommended a simple but consistent daily routine. Patients were more likely to stay relaxed when they could anticipate their day, and when they didn't feel rushed. That part should be easy, at least. Grandpa was a regimented person, so all they had to do was keep that going. The book suggested making a daily plan that covered everything from tooth-brushing to social activities. Even if they couldn't always completely stick to the plan, it would give Grandpa choices and allow him to stay involved in running his own life for as long as possible. And careful scheduling could minimize the confusion and mood swings that often came on later in the day—a common Alzheimer's side effect called "sundowning," which Archie was grateful to understand better.

There were tips about making the house

safer—installing handrails, avoiding trip hazards, placing locks on cabinets that contained anything potentially harmful. Thinking about a day when they might have to install locks made Archie sick to his stomach, so he skimmed over that chapter. It also recommended good fire safety, which would never be a problem in the house of a veteran fire-fighter. They practically had an extinguisher in every room.

Apparently certain uses of bright light could help an Alzheimer's patient sleep better. And music could help bring back memories that would otherwise be elusive.

The book didn't say anything about the power that stories could have. That didn't matter, though. Archie had done research online too—enough to know that scientists were exploring all kinds of treatments for Alzheimer's and that new findings were popping up all the time. If things as seemingly random as certain kinds of light and sound waves could have an impact, why not stories? Archie would never stop believing that the shared fantasies could slow the effects of the Alzheimer's. Just three days ago, he and Grandpa had repelled an alien invasion and saved Earth. Archie had woven in details from a Journal story about Grandpa's firehouse saving the wing of a hospital. It had only kept Grandpa lucid for a day, but still, that wasn't nothing.

His sleepy eyes finally processed what Mom was carrying. A tray with a glass of juice and a plate of eggs and toast. He frowned.

"Is he bad today?"

Mom shook her head. "Just a little shaky. I thought this would be better."

Grandpa never liked people waiting on him. That included serving him breakfast when he felt he could do it himself.

Archie buried his worry beneath a cheerful face. "Oh, okay."

"Hope school goes well. Make five good choices, then one terrible choice, just to keep 'em guessing."

Archie laughed. "I'll do my best."

With a smile, Mom moved farther down the hall. She tapped Grandpa's door with the corner of the tray and then slipped inside. "Hey, Dad."

Archie stood still, wondering if he should help. Mom's parting smile had been too tense to be genuine. The bus might wait a few minutes for him.

What are you going to do, spoon-feed him?

Good point, Me.

He started down the stairs. On the fifth step, he heard glass break.

He sprinted back to Grandpa's room and peeked around the doorframe.

"I'm sorry," Grandpa said. "Don't know how . . ."

Sitting in his favorite chair, he looked embarrassed as Mom scooped up pieces of glass and sopped up the spilled juice. This kind of thing seemed to be happening more frequently.

"No, no, it's fine, Dad," Mom said, her voice soothing and patient. "It's fine. Don't worry."

It was the first time Archie had seen Grandpa today. He understood now: *A little shaky* had been Mom's attempt to send him to school without this image in his head.

"Do you want to go anywhere today?" Mom asked. "Anywhere. You pick. I have to work, but I'm sure Violet can pick you up. And one of us will take you to the firehouse tonight like usual."

Grandpa stared into the middle distance. His attention had wandered that quickly, and not toward something nice. Archie could see it. Grandpa's expression was like a thin layer of stone on top of roiling lava, barely containing the chaos.

Archie's heart sank. It was a bad day.

Mom looked up from her cleaning. "Dad? Are you okay?"

Blinking, Grandpa saw her again. "Penny," he said. "Was I a good man?"

Mom's expression clouded. "Why would you ask that?"

"I just . . . well." He gripped the arms of his chair as if bracing himself. "There were days in the war. Bad days. Never talked about 'em, but right now, I can't stop remembering. I . . . did things. Made bad choices."

Archie stood thunderstruck. What was Grandpa talking about?

"They keep playing over and over, and . . ." He swallowed hard. "They make me wonder. About the man I was."

Alzheimer's was such a jerk, doing this to a man like Raymond Reese. Were the bad memories even accurate, or were they amplified and distorted by the disease? No wonder his rage kept resurfacing on bad days. What could a person say to make that better?

Mom put aside the broken glass and took Grandpa's hands in hers.

"Dad," she said. "I know there are things you regret. You may not remember, but you told me once about the war. About days when good choices weren't even possible. Those days don't cancel out the other choices you've made in your life. If I wrote down all the wonderful things you've done since—for your family, for your coworkers, for all the people you've helped—this house couldn't hold all the journals. That's the truth. That's what you have to remember."

So, whatever memory was plaguing Grandpa, Mom knew about it. Which meant it was probably real.

What had Grandpa done? Archie felt the overwhelming urge to sneak away and open the Journal, to tear through the forbidden pages until he found it. Only his promise kept him standing there.

Grandpa released a slow breath and sank back into his chair, the tension flowing out of him like steam. The turmoil under his expression seemed to settle. Squeezing Mom's hands, he smiled.

"You're a good daughter."

"And you're a great dad." She smiled back, then gathered up the tray and the broken glass. "Do you need anything else?"

"No, thank you."

"Okay. Give me ten minutes and I'll bring up a new tray."

"Thank you . . . Penny."

"You're welcome, Dad."

As Mom moved toward the door, Archie remembered that he'd been eavesdropping. He flinched back, caught between running downstairs and staying put.

Too late. Mom stepped into the hall and shut the door behind her. Closing her eyes, she sagged back against the wall and blew out a long breath. Exhaustion, grief, fear—they all rose to the surface now.

She hadn't noticed Archie. Gently as he could, he cleared his throat. Mom snapped back to attention, trying to recover the happy mask she'd worn before.

She got halfway there, but then the mask shattered. Her eyes filled with tears. Archie felt his own eyes burning. They stood there, sharing a look that held an entire conversation. This wasn't getting any easier.

"Is he going to be okay by himself today?" Archie asked.

"I . . ." She shook her head. "Zahira might be able to move some things around so I can take the morning off. If he's not doing better in a few hours, I'll see if Violet can come over this afternoon."

Archie knew that was only a temporary solution. He'd caught enough glimpses of the family text thread to know that Aunt Candace had suggested hiring someone to look after Grandpa, at least part time. But if this was how Grandpa was with his loved ones, Archie couldn't imagine how unsettled he'd be around a stranger.

Archie stepped closer and whispered, "He mentioned bad days during the war. What was he talking about?"

Now Mom's grief was laced with tension. Looking at Archie, she seemed to struggle with whether or not she should speak. Then she squared her shoulders, as if physically shaking it off.

"Grandpa is the man you've always known," she said. "Whatever happened decades ago doesn't change that."

"If that's true," Archie said, "why are you afraid to tell me?"

Mom's expression was inscrutable. Did she hold back just because Archie wasn't ready? Or because she believed it might change how he saw Raymond Reese?

Without answering, she turned toward her room. "Aren't you late for the bus?"

She was right. Though Archie burned to know more, he had to move. Once again, life wouldn't wait for him to be ready to face it.

~~~

The bell rang. Archie blinked.

Third period was over, and he barely remembered a word his science teacher had said. The same went for first and second periods.

Drifting through fog. That was how he felt today. Mechanically he gathered his things and headed for the door.

Zig caught up as he left. "Okay, we're definitely gonna have to quiz each other, or the next test will not be fun for me."

Archie grunted and kept walking, head down.

"You get any notes on that last part?" Zig continued. "It's wild. I mean, how can light be a wave *and* a particle? Man, I cannot wait for chemistry in high school. I might actually be able to use that in—"

"No," Archie snapped. "I didn't get notes. Like it matters."

Zig fell silent, and Archie felt like a jerk. None of this was his friend's fault. It was no one's fault.

Which felt worse, somehow. Just once it would have been nice to have someone to blame for all this.

"Tough morning, huh?" Zig said.

They reached their lockers. Archie tried to summon the will to move his arms.

Zig didn't open his locker either. He waited, supportive even in this small way.

"Yeah." Turning, Archie leaned back against his locker with a sigh. "Sorry, man."

Zig waved it away. "Don't sweat it."

"I . . . I feel like I'm watching him fade away. Mom can only do so much, and it's tearing her up. Sometimes I help with the disease, but lately that's been harder for some reason."

Archie almost brought up what he'd heard this morning, but something made him stop. Maybe because saying it out loud would make it real. Or maybe he just couldn't confess that, for the first time in his life, he had doubts about who his grandfather really was.

"You help with the disease?" Zig said.

"Yeah. You know, the fantasies that I act out with him. When I get it right, they hold the disease back. They sort of refresh Grandpa's memory and help him feel like himself again."

"Oh. Right. Um . . ."

Zig didn't finish the thought, so Archie glanced over at him. He wore a troubled look.

"What, Zig?"

Zig shrugged. "Nothing, bro. Whatever you're trying, I hope it keeps working."

He was holding something back. Archie didn't push it, though. Zig was trying to be supportive, so he decided to just be grateful. He should try being a good friend back.

"I'll find someone who took notes," Archie said. "Then quiz you till you pass out."

Zig laughed. "Deal."

Archie faked a laugh along with him. To his surprise, though, his arms weren't quite so heavy anymore. Maybe he could make it through the day after all. He turned to face his locker.

As he moved, the corner of his eye caught a familiar splash of color. Even peripherally, as a smudge in his vision, he would know it anywhere.

Desta was coming out of the art room, which was odd since she didn't have art class until later in the day. Then he saw the folder in her hands. Not the one that she brought to their project groups— the one that carried her sketches. Maybe she was doing something extra for art class. *Interesting.*

Archie thought back to the group meeting at his house—how Desta had made an observation that helped him with Mom. She'd seen something that Archie hadn't. Maybe he could do the same for her.

"Catch up with you later," he said to Zig.

"But your books . . ."

Archie dove into the stream of students moving to their next class. He weaved through them as fast he could without knocking someone over, until he caught up with Desta.

"Hey," he said.

"Hey, Archie," she said. "How was science?"

"Ask me after the next test," he replied. Desta laughed, which bolstered him to continue. "So, I wanted to thank you."

"What for?"

"You were right about my mom. Realizing that really helped."

"Things are better?"

"Yeah. Feels like we have each other's backs again."

"That's great, Archie. Really, I didn't do much, but I'm glad it helped. How's your grandfather?"

Archie's anxiety, momentarily forgotten, roared back to life. "Um, well, some days he's his old self. I just hope we can keep giving him those."

"I'm sure it means a lot to him that you try so hard."

Archie nodded his thanks, marveling once again at how much Desta cared, even about people she barely knew. He gestured at her folder. "Extra credit for art? Not that you need it."

"Extra lessons."

As they turned down a less crowded hallway, Desta flipped the folder open and showed him the top drawing. "Mrs. Matney's teaching me chiaroscuro shading."

"Ah, yes, churro shading," Archie said. "Sounds delicious."

Desta swatted his arm. "It's a real technique, and you'd better not eat my drawings."

"Well, stop making them sound like dessert."

Desta laughed. "I've also been sketching booth ideas for my project. Something to make being a surgeon seem more exciting."

"Come up with anything?"

She pursed her lips. "Maybe. I hope. There's only eight weeks left in the school year, and only *four* weeks until our essays are due. So that's not a lot of time to finalize things. Consider this a friendly push to choose your focus."

Archie hoped the embarrassment didn't show on his face. "I know. I mean, thank you. I really am trying."

"I know you are. Just remember we're here to help."

"Maybe I should just put every job I've thought of in a hat and pick one. That's a good way to choose a career, right?"

"Yes, if you're a cartoon."

"Wait, I can be a cartoon? Why didn't anyone tell me that?"

Desta grinned. "You're hopeless."

"Okay, then here's a promise. By the time our group meets again, I'll have a subject."

"Great! I'm excited to see what you come up with."

Archie started to say more, then hesitated. He needed to find the right words, like she had with him.

"Speaking of projects, I've been wondering— why do yours on medicine?"

"What do you mean?"

"It's just, you light up when you talk about art. Seems like that's what you really love."

"Sure, but art careers are a fantasy. My parents have always said so."

"Well, I mean, how do they know? Did they ever try?"

Oops. That was the wrong thing to say. Desta stiffened, her expression going stony.

"They have perspective that I don't," she said. "*Surgeon* is a real profession, and it contributes something to the world."

"Hey," he said gently. "If you end up really wanting to be a doctor, that's awesome. But you'll have years in high school and even in college to decide. So, why not talk about what you want to be right *now*?"

"Archie, it's just a hobby."

"Is that you talking, or your parents?"

Wrong again. Archie knew it the moment the words left his mouth. Desta's whole demeanor slammed shut like a steel door.

"I know they're just looking out for you," he added hurriedly. "But grown-ups all seem to have regrets. I just want you to be happy."

Desta's eyes softened a little at that, but Archie could tell he hadn't fixed the damage he'd done. She took a slow, deep breath, and he prepared himself to be verbally lit on fire.

"Thank you for your concern," she said, her tone formal and stiff. "But I've made my decision. I need to get to class now."

She strode away. Archie watched her go, wishing he had more feet so he could kick himself in the face.

Stupid stupid stupid stupid

Just then, flute music trilled over the intercom. Classroom doors clanged shut. Archie whipped around, realizing what he'd just done.

He'd walked to the opposite side of school from his next class. He'd left his books in the locker, and he'd just missed the bell for the start of fourth period.

Perfect.

Chapter 14

Archie shut the front door and tossed his backpack onto the nearest chair. One of the straps had broken during the bus ride home, causing most of his books to spill out of the half-zipped bag when it hit the ground. The cherry on top of an awful day.

At least Mom wasn't home from work. She always asked how his day was, and she could always tell when he held something back. Today there were stories he just did not want to tell.

There had better be something tasty in the fridge. Archie needed a distraction, even if it was momentary. He wandered into the kitchen in a cloud of his own troubles, only to find Grandpa sitting at the table with the Journal.

"Oh, hey."

"Hey, Fletch," he said. "Have a good day?"

"More or less."

Grandpa noted his expression. "Which was it?"

"What?"

"More good or less good?"

"Let's just say I look forward to forgetting this one. Hopefully soon."

A pained look crossed Grandpa's face. Then Archie realized what he had just said and who he was talking to.

"Aw, man." Shutting the fridge door, he dragged himself over to the table and plopped down across from Grandpa. "Sorry. Bad joke."

"You don't need to tiptoe around me," Grandpa said. "I'm a big boy . . . um . . ."

Blinking, he broke eye contact, seeming embarrassed for some reason. Archie stared, puzzled about what was happening. Then he realized.

"It's Archie," he said.

Grandpa closed his eyes and nodded. "Right. I gotta start carrying a cheat sheet. I couldn't remember your grandma's name this morning either."

Though he joked, the frustration was still there. Archie wracked his brain for something else to talk about, but his thoughts kept going back to what he'd overheard that morning. Did he dare ask Grandpa about it? If he did, would he be sorry he'd asked?

The Journal rested in Grandpa's hands, open to one of the happy stories. Archie recognized it as one he'd read, and his eyes lit up.

"Catching up on old adventures?"

Grandpa's expression darkened. Archie's heart sank—he had chosen wrong again, like with everything else today.

"Still feel like I'm only remembering bad days. Hard choices. Friends lost," Grandpa said. "I just . . . needed to remember the good things."

Archie tensed. Was he about to learn what happened years ago? "Did it work?"

Grandpa hesitated, then nodded. "I faced what happened all over again. Remembered how I made peace with it so long ago. And reminded myself of the man I've tried to be ever since. This book helped me along. Without it, I might have been lost." Grandpa traced his hand affectionately down the Journal's open page. "I feel what's happening to me, Fletch. All my days—it's like they're in a burning house, and there's nothing I can do except watch as they turn to ash. I just wish the bad ones had burned first."

Archie struggled against the lump in his throat.

I will not cry in front of him. He searched for comforting words to share and found that he had none.

Shaking his head, Grandpa stood. His movements were sluggish, full of despair. "I need some fresh air," he said, and left through the back door.

They had seen days like this before. When Grandpa started to spiral emotionally, things would be very bad by the time he hit bottom. Whatever doubts he was facing about the man who'd been his hero, he couldn't let that happen. Not again. Not today. Archie felt desperation rising. He had to act quickly.

His eyes locked onto the Journal, open to a page he had read fifty times.

You said you'd do things differently.

I know.

Both Archie and Mom had promised they would be better about facing this in the real world. For Archie, part of that meant learning about Alzheimer's so he could help with more than just shared fantasies.

Right now, though, Grandpa didn't need medical facts. He needed to remember! And no doctor could do what Archie could.

It hasn't been working like before.

Shut up. I can do this!

Grabbing the Journal, Archie flipped feverishly through the pages that Grandpa had marked for him. There had to be something more he could use, some nugget of a memory he'd missed.

He flew through the pages once, then twice. On his third desperate search, the reality became clear. He had used every shred of the stories he was allowed to read, and a repeat shared fantasy would have less impact than a new one. Recycling even the richest material had never gone well.

Verging on panic, he glanced out the kitchen window. Grandpa wandered aimlessly around the backyard, staring down at the grass as if all the fight had drained out of him. If Archie didn't catch this now, the spiral could last for days.

What if, this time, the real Raymond Reese never came back?

Archie glared at the Journal. So few pages marked. Some other pages had to have good stories. Darker stories, maybe, but ones that could still help.

He didn't know any of them. Out of respect for Grandpa, he'd never even sneaked a peak at the forbidden pages. Now, though, it was for Grandpa's own good.

He headed for the back door, flipping through

forbidden Journal pages with every step. Scanning for a clue, any key words that would signal he'd found a story he could use. Something heroic or funny or . . .

There it was. Archie caught the names Schmitty and Cobb. All the stories about those guys were awesome.

It was a start. He could keep reading and make up the rest as the fantasy unfolded.

Hitting the backyard, he raced off in Grandpa's direction. This was going to work. He could feel it.

~~~

Archie's muscles strained to their limit. Sweat poured down his face, stinging his eyes. The intense heat made the air hard to breathe.

The building shuddered, falling prey to the fire one level at a time. Soon it would collapse.

Slaying that dragon months ago had been such a victory. They couldn't have known it had a mate. They couldn't have known the mate would seek revenge by burning the walled town to ash. It had launched its vicious attack before anyone had even noticed it diving out of the sky.

But it hadn't counted on Grandpa and Archie being there. Now this new dragon was defeated and the town evacuated. Much would burn, but the people would live to rebuild. Archie and Grandpa only had one building left to clear out: an old inn at the edge of town.

Almost everyone had escaped the wooden structure. Only three remained to be rescued. So, through sheer force of will, Archie held this escape route open while Grandpa, Schmitty, and Cobb dove back into the maelstrom to find them.

Somewhere among the flames he heard voices calling. Someone was drawing closer. He redoubled his efforts, bracing himself in the last doorway, holding it together for as long as he could.

With a heavy crack, the frame above his head splintered. He shoved it back into place, gritting his teeth as the heat scorched his hands. No one was dying today.

"Archie!"

Grandpa appeared at the far end of a flaming hallway, arms wrapped around two large bundles. Locks of dark hair spilled from the tops of each.

Archie sighed in relief. They had known finding six-year-old twins who hid when they were afraid would be nearly impossible. But "nearly impossible" was their specialty.

Grandpa dashed down the hallway, cutting through flames to reach Archie's side.

"Time to go," he said.

"Got it," Archie said. "And the others are right behind you?"

"Schmitty and Cobb went after the last man. They didn't come through here?"

"No." Quickly Archie added, "They must've gone out through the side exit before it collapsed."

They turned and dashed into the smoke-filled common room. Archie led the way with Grandpa following. He let himself smile. This was working! Grandpa was starting to act like his old self.

He had scanned the Journal entry just enough to get the idea of what happened. The station had gotten a call about a hotel fire—a big one—and Grandpa and his fellow firefighters had saved a lot of lives.

They must not have been able to save everyone, though. Archie hadn't read the last couple of pages yet, but someone must have died. Otherwise this would have been marked as a good story.

That was just like Grandpa. Saving most wouldn't

have stopped him from regretting that he couldn't save them all. So Archie was giving him that chance. Today, everyone would live.

Archie kicked open the front door, and he and Grandpa strode outside, trailing smoke. The twins' sobbing parents thanked them profusely.

"Get yourselves out of town," Archie ordered them.

"We will, sir," the father said.

"What about Seamus and your friends?" the mother asked.

Grandpa froze, staring at the woman with haunted eyes. "What?" he said.

"The others," she insisted. "Will you get them out?"

"They got out already," Archie said. "They must have."

"No, sir." The husband shook his head vehemently. "Side exit collapsed, we never saw 'em come out."

Archie's mind raced, a dark weight sinking into his stomach. The story wasn't supposed to go like this! He and Grandpa turned back to face the inn, its ancient wood groaning and hissing as the flames consumed it.

"They're still in there," Grandpa said heavily. "I'm going back in."

He strode through the door and disappeared into a billowing wall of smoke. Archie tried to fight down the panic surging through his veins. This was all wrong. How could it have gone wrong so quickly? He had laid out the story perfectly!

But these fantasies were never just his. They were shared for a reason, and maybe Grandpa needed this. So, squaring his shoulders against the heat, Archie shoved down his fear and dove back in.

He caught up at a collapsed section of the inn, where a doorway had once been. Flaming debris was piled high there now, blocking their path. Grandpa stared at the rubble as if it were an enemy he'd like to throttle.

"They came through here," he said.

"How?" Archie said. "Hadn't it already collapsed?"

"No," Grandpa said. "I'm sure of it."

His voice was far away, as if he were deep in thought. Staring at the obstacle in their path, his expression changed from aggression to concentration. Archie realized that he was remembering.

"There was a second room," he said, barely

audible over the roaring flames. "Just past this one, just before the side exit. A room they might have . . ."

Archie hadn't read this detail in the Journal. Was Grandpa making something up for the fantasy, or bringing back a real memory?

Grandpa took three steps backward. "If this is a fantasy, and if we're the heroes . . ."

"Grandpa, what—?"

"Then I can do this."

With a fierce cry, Grandpa charged forward and hit the debris at full speed. With a great crashing sound, he burst through in an explosion of splinters and flames.

Archie yelped in alarm and ran in behind him. Grandpa had tumbled to the floor after making it through. Now he struggled to get back up. Archie fell to his knees and grabbed one of Grandpa's arms to steady him.

"That was nuts," Archie breathed. "But awesome. How'd you know there was . . . ?"

He trailed off. Never in his thirteen years had he seen that look on Grandpa's face—as if his greatest fear and deepest despair had clashed together like a thunderhead. He stared ahead unblinking, transfixed by the horror of whatever it was that he saw.

Trembling and confused, Archie pulled out the Journal, flipped to the last page of the entry, and read all the way to the end.

And felt like he would throw up.

The Journal slipped from his hands as he looked up, now seeing what Grandpa saw.

Seeing that Schmitty and Cobb hadn't made it. The caved-in roof had taken the man they tried to rescue, and then the smoke had taken them. Trapped in this tiny room with no way out, they had run out of time.

Only minutes too late, Grandpa had found them.

"No. No no no no no no," Grandpa whispered, shaking his head over and over again. "Not again, please not again . . ."

Archie had to burst the bubble, break the fantasy, get them out. Desperately he pulled on Grandpa's arm.

"We have to go—"

"NO!"

Grandpa shoved him hard. Archie stumbled, tripping over an unseen obstacle, and fell backward.

Then he was lying on his back, and the man standing over him was not the man he knew. It was a shell of Raymond Reese, full of rage and despair, tears streaming down his face, fists clenched.

Snarling, he took a step forward, and for the first time in his life, Archie was afraid of his grandfather.

"You," Grandpa spat. "You did this."

"Archie?" A distance voice shouted. "Dad?"

The fantasy shattered as Mom raced through the open door of the utility shed.

"Oh my God," she said. "What happened?"

Grandpa whirled toward her.

"They're dead!" he shouted at her, at the sky, at the world. "THEY'RE ALL DEAD!"

Mom stood wide-eyed, caught between crises and clearly unsure which to handle first. Then she moved toward Archie and knelt at his side, angling to stay between her son and her father.

"Are you hurt?" she asked.

Archie shook his head. He knew he was fine physically. Nothing could be as badly broken as his heart. With that thought, his own tears finally welled up and spilled over, hot and relentless.

I can't do it. I can't fight the disease.

I failed him.

I failed us all.

Chapter 15

Archie couldn't stop shivering. Lying in bed, he cocooned himself in a thick blanket that did nothing to chase away the cold.

He would never forget the look in Mom's eyes as she tried to calm Grandpa down, and he would never forgive himself for being the reason. He curled up more tightly, holding his body together while his insides fell apart. What had he been thinking?

I was trying to save him.

Really? another part of him challenged. *You really believed a story could fight a disease?*

He really had.

Hadn't he?

Insisting that this radical idea was working. Ignoring the doubtful looks, the patient words from family and even from Zig. Recklessly pushing ahead even though the shared fantasies had slowly stopped bringing Grandpa back. Only now, in the wake of this disaster, could Archie allow himself to ask the right questions.

Were you really doing it for him? Or for yourself, because you were afraid to lose him?

The look on Grandpa's face came back to him. Archie suspected that look would haunt him forever. Over the past few months, Grandpa had lost his temper more than once, gotten aggressive in ways that were completely out of character. But nothing like this.

They're all dead.

The wording snagged in Archie's mind. All. Not both. Not just Schmitty and Cobb? Who else?

Archie stared at the Journal. What else lurked between the carefully marked entries, crowding out Grandpa's good memories, turning him into someone Archie didn't recognize?

He had to know. If he'd known about Schmitty and Cobb, this disaster wouldn't have happened. If there was more—if there was worse—he needed to be prepared.

~~~

A while later, a soft knock interrupted his thoughts. Archie knew who it was but didn't have the strength to move. Eventually the door opened, and he heard his desk chair creak as Mom sat.

"Hi," she said.

He kept his face buried, unable to look at her. His voice quivered as he spoke. "Is it true?"

"Schmitty and Cobb ran back into that hotel to save someone. The last person they knew they could reach. When your grandfather realized how long they'd been gone, he ran back in too." She hesitated. "He . . . found their bodies. They were already gone, but he pulled them out anyway. And he never forgave himself."

Archie clenched his fists. "And I made him remember it."

Mom didn't say anything. It was all the confirmation he needed.

"I won't do it again," he said, choking back tears. "Not ever. I promise."

"I know, Archie," Mom said. He could hear the struggle in her voice too. "I know. It was a beautiful *idea*, sweetheart. I hope you know that."

Maybe. But he meant what he'd said. Something had to change. He had to change. It was time to stop hiding in fantasies and face the real world.

Which meant he had to ask the next question too. Bracing himself, Archie sat up and looked Mom in the eye.

"And the . . . other memory. From the war. Is that true too?"

Mom looked confused at first. Then her eyes snapped to Archie's desk, where the Journal lay open to a page that hadn't been marked as safe.

Wearily, she pinched the bridge of her nose. "Please tell me you didn't read that. You promised him you wouldn't."

Archie stared at her, incredulous. "After what happened today, that's still what you think? The fantasy failed *because* of a memory no one wanted to tell me. If I'd known, I never would've tried to use that Journal entry. How did keeping it secret help anything?" He wasn't going to apologize for reading the entry without Grandpa's permission—not anymore. Some memories needed to be shared, no matter how hard they were. Just look what happened when they were kept secret. "If you don't trust me by now—"

"It wasn't about trusting you, Archie. That memory wasn't mine to share. And your grandfather has always had a hard time talking about it. He never even told your aunts." She grimaced, massaging her temples. "It's the reason he started writing the Journal. So he could deal with it."

This must be pulling her apart. Archie tried to make his voice calmer, to show her that he wasn't attacking her. "I said I'd stop with the fantasies, and I meant it. But that might not be enough. What if one day we're just talking, and I say the wrong thing? Trigger the wrong memory? For all I know, there could be a lot more stories that upset him enough to make him . . ."

He couldn't bear to finish that sentence.

Mom winced as if the thought caused her physical pain. Blowing out a heavy breath, she sat down on Archie's bed. "The disease is making it harder for him to . . . process his feelings, and control how he expresses them. He's probably going to have more outbursts, yes. That's not your fault or his. Please don't start doubting who your grandfather is. He's the same person you've known your whole life."

Archie wasn't able to catch the next words before they flew out of his mouth. "But did I ever really know him?"

Mom looked down at her hands, appearing to gather herself.

"Their orders said the village was full of soldiers in disguise, waiting to attack after they passed by," she explained. "So, to protect themselves, they rushed in first. It wasn't until it was over, and the smoke cleared, that they realized their information was wrong."

"And innocent people died," Archie said. "A lot of them."

"Yes."

"Do you think it's true that none of the soldiers knew?"

"Your grandfather believes someone high up, whoever gave the order, knew the truth. They chose to lie and let their soldiers live with the guilt. He was horrified when he found out what he'd really done. After that, he just wanted to protect people."

A realization hit Archie, a connection he had never made before. "Is that why he became a firefighter?"

Mom nodded. "He's never said this, but I think it's why he saved so many people without worrying about himself."

"Because he . . ." Archie struggled, but then forced himself to say it. "Because he's been making up for that day."

"The worst day of his life. It made him want—
need to be a better man."

Archie tried to respond. Instead, without knowing why, he started to cry. Mom was there in an
instant, and they clung to each other.

"Oh, Archie," she breathed. "He never wanted
this to be anyone else's burden."

"All this time . . . he . . ."

"He only ever wanted you to know the man
he became." Mom pulled back and looked into his
eyes. "He's still that man, Archie, even now that you
know more of his story."

Archie nodded, wanting to believe her. But in
his heart, there were ripples of doubt. For all of
Archie's life, Raymond Reese had been a super-
hero. In Archie's eyes, he stood as tall and true and
unshakeable as a skyscraper.

Did this change things? *Should* it change things?
Archie didn't have a clue, and he was too exhausted
to try figuring it out. So the doubt remained.

They stayed there for a long time. Crying sometimes, sitting in silence others, taking comfort from
each other's presence. Until eventually he fell into
exhausted sleep.

Chapter 16

Archie opened the resource book to the chapter his family needed today—the one that told them how to make the house safer for someone with Alzheimer's.

For the thousandth time, he pushed away thoughts of the Journal. Of that story, and the questions he couldn't keep asking himself. *Just get through today*, he told himself.

He wished there were a chapter with advice for family members who felt like they were slowly sinking into a volcano. He had looked for ideas online but hadn't found much: *Take breaks. Get plenty of sleep. See a therapist.* Which all sounded good in theory but wasn't so easy to put into practice.

He suspected that there weren't any easy solutions because every situation was different, and because it was going to be awful no matter what you did. So coping boiled down to finding ways to manage the stress—counting to three before responding to something frustrating, going for walks, eating healthier snacks. But there was no way to avoid the mental and emotional toll it was going to take.

Still, thinking about this stuff at all was progress. Though the incident on Friday had drained him, and left him with questions about Grandpa that weren't easily answered, it had still led to an important breakthrough. He was leaving the fantasies behind. At least that felt like the start of forward movement, which Archie was only now realizing he had lacked all these months.

"All right, we're heading out," Uncle Dan announced as he entered the living room with Grandpa in tow.

Archie quickly shut the book and tucked it out of sight. Sitting around him, Mom and the aunts put on bright smiles. Well, Mom and Aunt Violet did.

Uncle Dan gave Grandpa's shoulder a friendly slap. "Gotta get this old man a beer before he turns to dust."

"Don't make me put you in a headlock again," Grandpa said.

"Have fun," Mom said. "You're dropping Dad off at the firehouse after, right, Dan?"

"Yes, indeed."

"Be good, you two," Aunt Candace said.

"We will do nothing of the kind," Grandpa announced.

"Yes, how dare you," Uncle Dan said.

The two men chuckled as they headed out the front door. Just before closing it, Uncle Dan shot a covert look back at the family. He didn't like his part in all of this, but he would never show that to Grandpa. The two had always had a close friendship.

When the door shut, everyone got to their feet.

"We should have a few hours," Mom said. Since Grandpa wasn't driving himself anymore, they could count on him being gone for a predictable length of time.

"Let's get to work," Aunt Candace said grimly, as if they were heading into battle. "Archibald, thank you for the book pages you sent over. I printed copies for the rest of us." She handed sheets of paper to Mom and Violet. "I highlighted each person's tasks and added some tips I found in my own reading."

Mom and Aunt Violet would be installing handrails and covering electrical sockets. Aunt Candace

was in charge of installing locks on anything dangerous. Which left Archie to get rid of trip hazards that
they may have taken for granted before.

Now more than ever, Archie wished that life was
like a movie. If it were, then right now it would
cut to a montage of everyone working on the house.
Bittersweet music would play in the background, sad
but with an undertone of hope, and the work would
be hard but ultimately satisfying. Someone would
start crying, but then someone else would make a
joke, and the laughter would build until their work
turned into a game of tag or a water balloon fight.

But that didn't happen. Archie felt every agoniz-
ing minute drag by as he combed the house—tucking power cords close to the wall, putting away loose
rugs and the runner on the stairs, repositioning furniture, even picking up books that had been stacked
on the floor or hidden in surprising places.

Don't think, just move. He concentrated so hard
on the task that his brain started to hurt from avoiding what was really on his mind. That Journal entry.
The horrible day Grandpa had written about. He
had felt the shame in Grandpa's words. But did being
ashamed make it better?

Maybe he'd never find a real answer. Especially

now that everything Grandpa had done, everything he had been—good and bad—seemed to be slipping away. As Grandpa lost pieces of himself, his family lost those pieces too.

When he crossed paths with Mom or one of the aunts—or with Uncle Dan when he got back from dropping Grandpa at the station—he saw the same look in their eyes that he saw in the mirror. They slogged through their tasks like empty shells. They were stressed and on edge but trying to convince themselves that this was a good thing because they were being proactive.

None of this was a good thing for any reason. But if Archie stopped, if he let himself acknowledge that, he wasn't sure he'd be able to start again.

He found himself in Grandpa's room, tucking away trip hazards as gently and subtly as possible. If he changed too much, or rearranged anything important, it could disrupt Grandpa's state of mind for days.

A stack of old photo albums lay precariously close to the edge of their shelf. He set them right, making note of their location so he could come back and search for interesting photos later. Maybe they contained happy memories he could share with Grandpa.

His stomach dropped. The thought had occurred to him out of lifelong habit. Would sharing memories with Grandpa ever be the same again?

Archie stepped back, bumping against the easel next to the window. With a wooden clatter, it half-folded and began to topple. He just managed to grab it and save Grandpa's latest painting from plopping facedown on the carpet.

As he fixed the easel and reset the artwork, he examined it for smudges. Looking at the canvas from this close, he realized this piece looked familiar. Hadn't he seen something like it before?

Archie crossed the room and flipped through a series of Grandpa's finished paintings, chasing a vague hunch until he found it. Old canvas in hand, he walked to the easel and held it up beside the new one.

Grandpa's fire station. Both paintings showed the building from the same angle. Except, where the old painting was focused, with sharp lines and bright colors and a strong sense that this was a real place, the new painting was different. The lines were blurry and wavy, the colors muted, the sky mottled, like a dreamscape version of a place that the artist had only heard about but never actually seen.

Or like a place the artist could barely remember.

With a heavy sigh, Archie put the old painting back where he'd found it. Suddenly, he couldn't bear being in this room any longer. He scoured the rest of the house for clutter, moved or braced any furniture that might tip over, and did his best not to touch any of Grandpa's favorite things.

Finally, after about three eternities, he was finished. While his family put finishing touches on their assignments, he retrieved the Journal and sat in the living room.

After a day like this, he could use a good memory, even if he'd read it a dozen times. Even if it was adjacent to dark memories that Grandpa had spent a lifetime trying to get past. So he opened the book to read about the day Grandpa had met Grandma.

It happened at the tail end of young Raymond Reese's postwar travels. After he arrived back in the country via Los Angeles, he ended up somehow being a background stunt performer on a low-budget movie that never got released. On the movie set, he met a young production assistant named Ella Scott, and family history was made. Soon after they had fallen in love, Grandpa confessed to missing the green foothills of Missouri and they made plans to—

"What are you reading?" Aunt Candace demanded.

Archie flinched and looked up. He'd been absorbed in the story and hadn't noticed his family coming into the living room. Why did Aunt Candace sound like she was accusing him of something?

"Um, Grandpa's Journal?" he said.

"And what makes you think it's okay for you to read that?"

"Grandpa gave it to me."

"No, he didn't. Give that to me right now."

"He really did, Candace," Mom said.

"Oh, were you there? Or did Archie tell you he did?"

Archie bristled. "Don't call me a liar."

Suddenly, the air was thick with tension.

Uncle Dan leaned toward his wife and spoke softly. "Babe, that's a little harsh. Why would he lie?"

"Dad's own *daughters* never got to read that!" Aunt Candace snapped. "Suddenly it skips a generation to the boy?"

Mom rolled her eyes. "This isn't a gender issue. Come on. Our mother read it all the time."

"Wasn't that book part of Dad's therapy?" Aunt Violet said. "That's, like, a really private thing. He doesn't have to share it with anyone."

Aunt Candace glared at Archie. "And yet he gave it to someone who hasn't earned it."

Mom's back went stiff. She aimed a stony look at her younger sister. "That's not fair, Candace, and you know it."

Aunt Candace looked away.

Archie clamped his mouth shut, afraid of what he might say. He tried to appear calm, but inside his blood was boiling. He hadn't earned this? He lived with Grandpa every day, helped him every day, watched him deteriorate *every day*. Where was Aunt Candace every day?

The room filled with a silence that could melt steel.

Uncle Dan placed a comforting hand on Aunt Candace's knee. "Think about your dad," he said. "He's old school. He would want his kids to see him as bulletproof, as their protector, and writing that journal is probably the most vulnerable thing he's ever done. You can understand that, right?"

"I would hope so," Mom said. "In that way, Candace, you're more like Dad than any of us."

"And it's not like he hasn't told us most of those stories over the years," Aunt Violet said. "If I had to choose between Dad and a book, I'd rather keep the memories of talking to Dad, all the way from our childhood to now. Archie won't have as many of those memories."

Trust me, you wouldn't want to know every story, Archie almost said. He clenched his jaw to keep quiet.

For the first time, a shadow of regret crossed Aunt Candace's face. She drew in a deep, shaky breath.

"I'm sorry, Archie," she whispered.

There was still fire in Archie's veins. He almost snapped back with something less than forgiving. But then he saw her lip quiver, and then her tears began to fall.

She swiped them away. "I just miss him already."

Archie couldn't remember ever seeing her cry before. It was easy to forget that Aunt Candace was a real person with feelings that ran as deep as theirs. Which meant she was hurting just as much.

Standing, Archie crossed the room and held out the Journal. "I would want to know too."

Aunt Candace stared for a moment, then shook her head and gently pushed the Journal back toward him. "I . . . I think Violet's right. I love my memories of Dad the way they are now. Maybe I should keep them that way. And you deserve to have your own memories of him, Archie." She huffed, fresh tears falling. "I just feel so helpless."

There was a sniffle behind Archie. He turned to see Aunt Violet crying softly now.

"He always said we would need each other one day," she said.

Then she was on her feet, and so was Aunt Candace, and they were hugging each other tightly. Mom joined the hug as her own tears came, clutching a sister in each arm.

By the time Uncle Dan and Archie got swept into the group hug, they were one big mass of tears. Archie could barely tell where he ended and the next person began, and there was no knowing how long it lasted.

Eventually, they had cried enough for the moment, but no one let go.

"So," Uncle Dan said, sniffling. "Who's ready to start drinking? Just chocolate milk for you, Archie."

That made them all laugh. Archie savored the relief of having something—anything—to smile about.

"I'm so glad you're all here," Mom said. "If we have to face this future, at least we can do it together."

Chapter 17

Facing the future apparently meant getting up like normal the next morning.

"Come on, move it," Mom said with forced cheer. "It's a new day, and we're both going to make it awesome."

Then she pelted Archie with balled-up pieces of paper from his desk until he got out of bed, said good morning, and promised to be awesome. Even *pretending* he wasn't emotionally ravaged helped him feel a bit better. Enough to be functional, anyway. Enough to get ready and catch the school bus on time.

He was also beginning to see how the fantasies had made him feel so powerful. So fearless. Only when he lost that power—even though it hadn't been real—did Archie realize how little he could actually help his family.

As soon as he stepped off the bus, Zig caught up with him. "Hey, bro."

Archie gathering meager scraps of energy and prepared to channel them into being cheerful. He faced Zig with a big smile.

Zig stopped short. "Whoa. Dude, are you okay?" His eyes went wide as saucers. "Is your gran—?"

Archie laughed. Of all his friends, only Zig could see through him so easily.

"Rough night," Archie said as they walked through the front doors of Blue Sun Academy. "I'll probably be kinda off today."

"Well, whatever you need, just say the word."

"Thanks, man."

On the way to his locker, he happened to walk past Desta, who gave him a small, strained smile but didn't say hi. Oh, right—he'd messed up badly with her too. With everything that had happened over the weekend, he'd almost forgotten about Friday's conversation. Another thing he didn't know how to fix.

Archie hoped his homeroom would be quiet. Maybe he could grab a quick nap before the day started in earnest.

Instead he was confronted with the sight of Spencer Harrington perched atop a desk, regaling his classmates with the tale of his latest athletic triumph, which had singlehandedly won the baseball game last night. Apparently, there were no other players involved, or even on the team.

". . . they had no idea what hit 'em . . . I ran like lightning, they couldn't touch me . . . I tagged like twenty guys out . . ."

Archie plopped into his seat, working to ignore the flood of me-me-me's pouring from Spencer's mouth. He pulled out a textbook, realized it was the wrong one, and leaned over to dig in his bag.

"Gotta be all the weights I'm lifting. Seriously, I could, like, lift a truck. Who wants to arm wrestle me?"

Archie went still, waiting for someone to accept the challenge. Hoping one of his classmates would step up. Spencer wasn't the only jock in their homeroom, after all.

But all was quiet. Archie abandoned his bag and sat upright. Spencer's circle of admirers glanced sheepishly at each other, while Spencer sat above them with a superior smirk.

He flexed. "Come on, no one's got the guts?"

Archie wondered the same thing. Even if someone lost, just accepting the challenge would be a win. It would show Spencer that not everyone was intimidated by him.

Grandpa always said, *Words are cheap. Actions are gold.*

And Spencer loved his words. Someday, though, they wouldn't be enough to get him what he wanted. Someday, someone would shove them back in his face.

Someday . . .

Someone . . .

Spencer laughed. "Still the king."

Before Archie knew what was happening, he had stood and walked to the edge of Spencer's circle.

"I'll do it," he said.

Spencer scoffed. "'Scuse me?"

Archie bristled. He might not be the athlete Spencer was, but he had always been strong. And he'd had enough of Spencer's bragging.

"You heard me," Archie said.

Spencer shook his head. "Dude, be serious. I'll destroy you."

"Maybe," Archie said.

"So sit back down."

A fire ignited inside Archie. "Why? You scared?"

A chorus of *oooooh*s went up from the other

students. Spencer's sarcasm melted. He stared hard at Archie. A moment later, they were facing each other across Spencer's desk, arms up and hands locked together.

Why are you doing this? He brushed the thought away. Spencer had been given every advantage his whole life. He was even planning a future where he would take credit for other people's hard work. *Let's see his parents' money get him out of this one.*

Another jock—a football player, Archie, thought—wrapped his hands around Archie's and Spencer's.

"All right, you two, I want a clean match," he said with a referee's tone. "No poking each other in the eye, or however they cheat in arm wrestling. Cool?"

They both nodded.

"Cool," the football player said. "Try not to break his arm, Spencer."

"No promises," Spencer said, his eyes locked onto Archie.

Archie kept his expression neutral. Inside, though, he felt a wave of anxiety. Why choose today, of all days, to do this? Because he wanted to add humiliation to the list of reasons this week was the worst?

No. Because, eventually, someone has to face the dragon.

Latching on to that thought, using it to focus, Archie flexed his hand and regripped it around Spencer's. After getting a rock-solid hold, he squeezed.

A flash of shock registered on Spencer's face.

The football player released. "GO!"

Archie tensed his arm and the rest of his body. Spencer shoved against Archie's arm with staggering force. Not just trying to win, but trying to humiliate him by winning as quickly and powerfully as he could.

Here came the embarrassing end Archie had feared. He would just have to take comfort in having challenged the dragon at all.

Except . . . Archie's arm wasn't moving.

His anxiety turned to elation. While Spencer trembled with effort, Archie held them both in place. It was actually kind of easy.

Spencer was starting to look panicked. It was clear what was going to happen. Archie was going to win. Easily.

Letting himself smile just a little, Archie moved his arm forward one inch. Then two. Then three. With each advancement, he watched Spencer's hope diminish. The roar of the onlookers barely registered in his ears. There was only the battle.

Who's the king now, Spencer?

Everything inside Archie screeched to a halt. That thought wasn't like him. Why would he say something like that, even in his own head?

Again, he made himself ask the question: Why was he doing this, and why today?

Staring across the desk at Spencer, Archie finally understood. Because, after yesterday, he had never felt more powerless in his life.

Grandpa was slowly leaving him—in more ways than one now. There was nothing he could do about it, and there never had been. So he'd seized this chance for a real battle. A way to vent all his frustrations on the world.

Archie saw true fear in his opponent's eyes. To his utter disbelief, Spencer's bottom lip trembled. Did the thought of losing actually put him on the verge of tears?

Spencer Harrington came into focus now, and Archie saw him for what he really was. Not a villain, certainly not a dragon, but a boy with a paper-thin ego desperately clinging to a shred of glory like it was all he had.

In a flash, this no longer mattered.

You've already won, he told himself. *You know it, and he knows it. Anything more would be just to humiliate him.*

Is that the kind of person you want to be?

The Archie of a few months ago, even a few days ago, would have raged against that. Didn't someone like Spencer deserve to be humbled? But the Archie of today—who was trying to be the kind of person that Grandpa had worked so hard to teach him to be—knew better.

It didn't matter if he won. It mattered how he won, and winning this way would only feed his own ego with the wrong kind of pride. The kind that was really poison.

So, steeling himself, Archie leaned forward and whispered so that only Spencer could hear under the cheers of their audience.

"It's a tie," he said.

Spencer frowned, disbelieving. "What?"

"We're stuck." Archie flicked his eyes significantly at their hands. "You can't move, and neither can I."

Spencer stared at him. "But you're . . ." he began, then trailed off without saying what they both knew.

"I'm serious," Archie said. "You with me?"

Spencer considered, and then nodded.

"Okay," Archie said. "Three. Two. One."

Archie and Spencer released their grips. The cheering gave way to a collective gasp.

"What was that?" their referee demanded.

Eyes still locked with Spencer's, Archie shook his arm as if getting the tension out. "Tie game," he said.

For a moment, Spencer didn't respond, and another spike of anxiety hit Archie. Had he just condemned himself to . . .?

"Yeah, we're dead even," Spencer said. "He got me a little bit, though." Then he stood, offering his hand. "Good match, bro."

As if in a dream, Archie rose and accepted Spencer's hand. A significant look passed between them. One that said they both understood what had happened here and that even held a hint of respect.

"Yeah," he said. "You too."

Chapter 18

Three days passed. Three days of Archie half-sneaking around his own house, flinching at every creak in the floor.

Grandpa had drifted in and out of lucidity ever since the . . . the bad day. Archie saw him fluctuate, but from a distance. He'd been steering around his grandfather, making himself scarce in subtle ways that he hoped no one would notice.

The house was quieter now to keep distractions to a minimum. Grandpa's daily activities, and his heaviest meal, were moved from evening to afternoon, when he was the most aware. The family took turns going on walks with him, trying to keep his body and mind active. Aunt Candace was almost ready to hire a nurse, which should help relieve some pressure.

Archie just needed space and time to himself. Time to think, to adjust to all these changes, to figure out how he really felt about what he'd learned. Whenever that space began to shrink, his anxiety skyrocketed.

It didn't help that the next project meeting drew ever closer and Archie still had no clue what to do. He'd begun to fear he was doomed to a life of flailing around, never able to make a decision or pick a direction. His friends would all go off to careers and families and he'd just be standing there, shrugging.

So, once again, he'd turned to books for inspiration. But instead of burying his head in fantasy, Archie had checked out two biographies from the library—one about J. R. R. Tolkien, the other about Alex Haley. He'd just finished the Tolkien bio and was starting on Haley's now. He absorbed every detail he could in search of lessons for his own life. All that nervous energy meant he couldn't sit still, so he found himself slowly walking while he read. Only a small piece of his mind was aware of his body wandering around the yard and then through the house, turning page after page until—

"Hey, Fletch."

Archie flinched, nearly dropping the book. He'd wandered into the kitchen without realizing it. One look at Grandpa's face revealed that this was a very good day. The old Raymond Reese sat at the table, eating a snack.

"Oh," Archie breathed. "Hi."

Anxiety roared back, buzzing through him like hornets. Archie glanced left and right, fighting the urge to close the book and run somewhere. Anywhere.

It must have shown on his face. Grandpa watched, his own expression pinching. To anyone else, it would have been imperceptible. To Archie, it was like seeing an open wound. Great—now he'd hurt Grandpa, and he could add guilt to the list of feelings to deal with.

Looking unsure, Grandpa gestured to the chair across from him. His voice was almost pleading. "Sit with me? Just for a little bit?"

Archie complied, willing himself to relax and only partially succeeding. Grandpa stared down at his hands for a long moment. Long enough that Archie wondered if they were going to just sit there in silence.

"I know you read the Journal entries," Grandpa finally said.

Archie's whole body tensed.

Looking at him now, Grandpa held up a hand. "It's okay. After what happened, I would've done the same." He pursed his lips in concern. "How are you feeling about it?"

Archie sat back, caught off guard. It was such a simple, direct question—one that nobody had asked him in a while. "I—well, I mean, it was . . . but you're *you*, and so I . . ." Archie shook his head. Even he had no clue what he was trying to say. "I mean, it was so long ago. Does that change, or—I mean, should it . . ."

He gave up with a shrug, and then his shoulders sagged in defeat. He stared down at the table. For a quiet moment, Grandpa only watched. When he did speak, his voice was soft.

"But it was not easy to pretend, anymore, that he was a hero in a story."

Archie recognized the quote from *The Eye of the World* by Robert Jordan, the first book in a series he and Grandpa had shared.

"A good person says what he means, Fletch, and he does what he says. If he makes mistakes, he owns up to them, and tries to do better next time," Grandpa said. "He does it even when it's hard. Even when he's afraid. I've told you that before, and I know it's true because . . . because I've learned it the hard way."

Archie looked up at him, unsure how to respond.

"I don't blame you for having doubts," Grandpa continued. "I did, every time I looked at myself in the mirror. I used to stare at myself and think, *Why didn't you ask more questions? Why didn't you make sure those orders were right, no matter who gave them?* They may have pointed the gun, but I pulled the trigger. And now I live with those memories because I can't go back and change them. All I can do is move forward and make better choices, and I've been trying to do that ever since."

He turned to gaze out the window, at the golden afternoon light filtering through the trees. A tear fell from his eye.

"I won't pretend I've left that day behind, because I never have. I never wanted to. It reminds me of the person I worked to become afterward. Pushed me to be that person every day, to be a force for good. A shield instead of a sword. I . . ."

He trailed off. Swallowing hard, he cleared a lump from his throat.

"I would have told you myself, soon. I only regret that you learned it from a book and not from me, and at the worst possible time. But I don't regret that you know."

He turned back, meeting Archie's eye.

"I tried to be an example as you grew up. Tried to teach you, in the best ways I knew, to care about others, to value honesty and kindness and fairness, to do the right thing even when it's hard or scary. And if I'm honest, it felt good to see you looking up to me. So maybe I tried too hard to hide my own mistakes. Maybe I accidentally taught you that being a good person was the same as being perfect. If I did, that's on me. You were always going to learn at some point that *no one* can be perfect."

Grandpa smiled wistfully.

"And yeah, I'm . . . I'm embarrassed that you know my worst failures. Ashamed, even. But in an odd way, I'm glad this happened now, before I forget myself completely. At least this way, we can talk through it together, help it all mean something."

Archie felt like he should say something comforting or understanding. It wasn't that he didn't want to. It was just—what *could* he say? How should he say it?

Grandpa must have seen his dilemma. With a nod, he stood. "You're smarter and stronger than I was at your age, Fletch. I know you'll come through this the right way. However you end up feeling—about all of it—I trust you, and I understand." He turned to leave, then hesitated. "You're my hero too, you know."

Archie's jaw fell open. *What?*

When Grandpa had disappeared upstairs, Archie sat alone at the kitchen table, trying to make sense of everything he'd heard. Doing the right thing had always seemed simple to him. But if Grandpa could get so tangled up, then maybe choosing the right path wasn't always so easy. Maybe even a good person could get lost.

Archie couldn't sit still any longer. Leaving the biography behind, he started walking again. While his mind focused inward, his body wandered into the woods behind the house and followed the path of the creek.

Fragmented feelings swirled around him, within reach but hard to grasp. So much to process. Too much. How was he supposed to feel? He didn't have a clue.

But maybe it didn't matter how he was supposed to feel. Maybe what mattered was how he *did* feel, knowing the whole truth now about the man he'd spent his life idolizing.

Archie sat on a smooth, flat rock. Eyes fixed on the rushing water, he turned his vision inward. He pried open his own heart, forcing himself to look at it—really look at it—maybe for the first time.

No surprise: his first thoughts were about stories. Even in fantasy, perfection was boring. It never felt right. The most interesting heroes were always the ones who struggled. Who made mistakes but kept trying.

But you've held him to a different standard, haven't you?

Archie knew it was true. He'd always seen Grandpa as infallible. And ever since learning the full story, Archie had wondered if his hero was someone he could no longer look up to.

But all those flawed heroes in all those stories— didn't he respect them more for learning from their mistakes and not giving in to their darkest days? Didn't he admire them for working to become better people?

Hadn't Grandpa done the same thing?

Archie's thoughts turned to these past months. To the setbacks, but then to the unexpected successes, and to the ways he'd grown through it all. Life at home got harder and more tangled as Grandpa got sicker, but other parts of life were getting better.

Archie's bond with Mom was stronger than ever. School life was improving, and his friendships were deepening.

The more he pondered, the more closely he looked at all of it, the more clearly Archie saw a common thread. Everything was connected.

In a flash, it all came together: how he felt about Grandpa's past, and what he wanted to do with his own life going forward.

Now he knew what to do about Desta.

And he had just found his project.

Chapter 19

Archie darted up to the little red coupe and slid into the passenger seat.

"Archie! What's up?" Zahira Bakshi, the receptionist from Mom's dental office, said from the driver's seat. She held out her fist. "I'ma need you to bump this right now."

Archie bumped her fist. "Hey, Zahira. Thanks for doing this. Without you, I would've had to ask Mom or my study group for a ride, and that would've ruined the surprise."

"You got it. I mean, I get to help you do something awesome *and* keep a fun secret from Penny? I seriously would've paid money to do this."

Archie laughed. "I'm glad. You know where it is, right?"

"Yep, heading there now."

"Thanks. So how's college?"

"Psh, the wooooooooorst. So much work, and all the teachers are straight-up *obsessed* with grades. Good thing I'm a genius."

They passed the time driving with more banter. Zahira was the least serious person Archie had ever met. If she became his dentist someday, he might actually look forward to getting his teeth cleaned.

Before he knew it, they were easing to a stop at their destination. Staring out the window, Archie felt a flash of nerves. He had been so certain until this moment, but now he hesitated.

Zahira poked him playfully. "Pretty sure you have to go *inside* the building."

"I just want this to go right," he confessed. "What if they won't help?"

"Dude, if half of what I've heard about your grandfather is true, they'll be falling over each other to do whatever they can. You just have to get in there and ask."

Archie nodded. "You're right. Even if it doesn't work, I still have to try."

"Totally. And hey, if it doesn't and you decide you can't face your classmates, we can always run off and get married."

Archie laughed and opened the car door. "Thanks. I'll be back soon—but hopefully not *too* soon."

Stepping out onto the sidewalk, he stared up at the firehouse—Grandpa's old firehouse—and made himself stand taller. At least half the people inside had been trained by Raymond Reese. If they were willing to help with Archie's plan, it would mean everything.

~~~

"Ramen's almost ready," Zig announced. "Remember, honest feedback is how a chef improves."

Desta sniffed the air. "It smells . . . mysterious."

Zig smiled. "I'll take it! This recipe is kind of an experiment."

The group sat around Desta's dining room table once again. For the first time, Archie looked forward to the session without the usual dread. Finally, he had his own project to share.

Though that was only one of his goals. He sneaked a glance at Desta. She had been polite since that disastrous conversation, but there was a wall between them now. If he handled things right today, hopefully that would change.

"Kam," Desta said, "you've got good news. Want to start us off?"

"For sure." Eyes bright, Kamiko looked to Archie. "Your idea totally worked. I wrote my essay from the perspective of a shelter dog getting adopted and sent it to the volunteer coordinators of my favorite shelters, and two of them loved it! So instead of *no* shelters, now I'm working with two."

"That's great!" Archie said.

"Yeah, I'm totally stoked. Now the real work begins." She opened her project folder, which was twice as thick as the last time Archie had seen it. "Logistically, I'm putting together something like an animal clinic and a petting zoo at the same time. It'll be a challenge to fit in the animals, a petting area, and a vet tech station. We'll need to keep the area clean and the animals fed. I need to set it up so people can adopt an animal right there, which means paperwork. And before all that, I have to clear everything with the event center."

"They'll probably need to put our booths far apart," Zig said. "Since I'm serving food and you'll have live animals."

"Right, good point." Kamiko clicked her pen and jotted down a note. "So, yeah, it's a ton of work,

229

but I'm happy I get to do it." She looked to Desta. "You made some progress too, right?"

"Yes." Desta patted her own project folder. "Oncology. I'm going to be a surgeon for cancer patients. I couldn't figure out what to demonstrate, so instead I'm finding real-life stories of people whose lives were saved by cancer surgeons. I'll print some out, then have my laptop playing video interviews."

"Wow," Zig said. "Cancer surgeon. That's a big deal. Are you making those stories part of your essay?"

Desta pursed her lips. "I'm still not sure. Nothing feels right for the essay so far."

Archie's heart leapt. He cleared his throat, not sure how Desta would react to a suggestion from him. "I, um, might have an idea."

When their eyes met, Desta's expression was perfectly pleasant, but Archie could still feel the awkwardness underneath. He pressed ahead.

"What if you wrote a journal entry from your future self? Like it's a day when someone lived because you were able to save them. Maybe you see them reunited with their family. Something that shows your hopes about the career, not just the nuts and bolts of it."

Desta tilted her head and stared into the middle distance for an eternal moment. Archie realized that he was holding his breath, and that he should probably stop doing that.

"That could work," she said finally. "Thank you, Archie."

To avoid bursting with joy, Archie kept his mouth clamped shut and just nodded.

"Spencer, you want to go next?" Desta said. "You were going to research what charity boards to sit on."

Spencer had been unusually quiet, listening more than he spoke. "I'm, uh, not doing that anymore."

Eyebrows rose all around the table.

"Really? Why?" Kamiko asked.

"Because of you, actually. When we were at Archie's, you talked about wanting to be a vet because it meant actually doing something, helping out directly. I hadn't thought about that before, and it made sense. So, now I'm looking at something a little more . . . hands-on."

Archie didn't know what to think. Even now, Spencer was being a little dramatic, but he wasn't showboating to the extent he normally did. Curious.

"What kind of hands-on?" Zig asked.

"Still environmental charity—or, more like environmental justice. You'll see what I mean. I'm redoing my whole presentation, but it should be ready by project night." Then Spencer shocked Archie even more by turning to him. "You want help picking a topic? Let's get it done."

With a knowing smile, Zig stood. "I've heard about this already, so I'll bring the ramen."

As Zig retreated to the kitchen, Archie worked to mentally pick his jaw up off the floor. He was still recovering from hearing the words "environmental justice" come out of Spencer's mouth, followed by what had sounded like a halfway sincere offer of help.

"Actually, I chose something," Archie said. "For real this time."

"Awesome," Kamiko said. "Tell us about it."

"Well, I'm keeping a lot of details quiet so the surprises don't get back to my family. But there's one thing I do need your help with." From his project folder, he pulled a sheet of paper showing the layout of the exhibit hall. "I know what I want to display, but not how to display it. Maybe we could kick around some ideas after we eat."

As he spoke, Zig reappeared and began handing

out bowls of steaming ramen. "Don't wait for me—eat up while it's hot." Zig said before ducking back into the kitchen.

Archie's mouth was already watering. Picking up a spoon, he scooped up the broth and took a taste.

He froze. Not because he was overwhelmed by delicious flavor. Because his whole body was rejecting the soup.

He forced himself to swallow, then glanced up from his bowl to sneak a look at everyone else. Maybe it was just him. Maybe he was missing the brilliance of . . .

. . . nope. Everyone was turning green.

Spencer looked like he was struggling not to spit out his first spoonful. "Sweet beard of Zeus," he whispered. "That's the worst thing I've ever tasted."

"This soup is a crime," Kamiko said before chugging her soda.

"Sure is quiet in there," Zig called from the kitchen. "Hope that's a good sign!"

Desta shot Archie a panicked look. "You're his best friend. What should we say?"

"I have no idea! I'm still shocked he's capable of making something this gross," Archie moaned, nearly gagging. "Sshh, he's coming!"

At that moment, Zig came back. They all managed to put on neutral faces as he sat down at his own bowl and picked up a spoon.

"Hey, Zig," Archie said, overly casual. "What's in this?"

"Pineapple and liver. Never seen it done before, so I thought I'd give it a shot. I mean, all the great chefs take risks, right?"

Archie couldn't bear to respond. The group sat in silence as Zig scooped up a spoonful and put it in his mouth.

The silence stretched as Zig rolled the soup around in his mouth, testing the flavor, slowly chewing the little chunks of pineapple and liver. He glanced up at the ceiling, deep in thought. Then, as if he'd come to a decision, he set down the spoon and folded his hands together.

"Well," he said. "That may be the grossest thing I've ever tasted."

The others expelled a chorus of relieved sighs. Then sighs became laughter as the tension melted. And no one was laughing harder than Zig.

"Your faces when I walked in!" he said through full-on belly laughs.

He took mercy on them and cleared away the

bowls, announcing that his earlier attempt at ramen would be on the menu for project night. To say it was the right decision would have been a massive understatement.

An hour later, everyone was packing up. It seemed like they had momentum now, both individually and as a group. It felt good.

Archie's phone chirped—a text from Mom. She was waiting outside in the car.

Which meant it was now or never. He had one more thing to do tonight. So, while his heart raced, he said goodbye to the group and then subtly approached Desta.

"Mind walking out with me?" he said quietly.

She still had her shields up. After a slight hesitation, she nodded and walked with him toward the foyer.

Archie felt the sudden urge to run. He tried to think of a story where a guy apologizes to his dream girl, but he drew a blank. Why hadn't books prepared him better for this? She was almost at her front door now, but he'd forgotten all the words he knew.

Then he remembered some. Not his own words, but the words he needed in this moment.

A good person says what he means and does what he says. If he makes mistakes, he owns up to them and tries to do better next time. He does it even when it's hard. Even when he's afraid.

He braced himself. "I owe you an apology."

Desta's eyebrows rose.

"You gave me great advice about my mom," he continued. "So I wanted to help you too. But my advice about your project kind of . . . well, it was awful, and I was way too pushy about it."

Desta's shoulders relaxed and her expression softened. "Your advice wasn't awful. Maybe a little, um, insistent, but I know you were just trying to help."

"I was. But I kind of assumed I knew everything about you, when I really don't."

"No, you . . . you knew more than I wanted to admit." She opened the door and stepped outside. "Not even my parents saw what you did. Or maybe they just didn't want to. I mean, art isn't exactly a safe career."

Archie nodded as they walked down the driveway. "I get it. It's their job to protect you."

"Yeah. But maybe sometimes they confuse safe with happy. I don't think they're the same thing."

They were halfway to the car. Archie knew he

didn't have long. "I'm glad you're not mad," he said. "But still, I think I hurt your feelings. That was wrong, and I'm sorry."

Desta shot him an appraising glance. "A guy who can admit he's wrong. I like that."

Archie's insides burst like fireworks. "Well, um, I'm wrong a lot."

He winced, mentally kicking himself. Mercifully, Desta laughed and gave him a playful shove. They stopped next to his mom's car.

"I'm glad you found your project. We were all rooting for you. Good night, Archie." With a little wave, she turned and walked back up the driveway.

"See you soon," Archie said. He lingered there for a moment. He could still smell her shampoo.

Before she could turn and catch him looking, he opened the car door and climbed inside.

"Good study session?" Mom asked.

As the car pulled away, he glanced back. Desta had stopped at her door and half-turned to watch them leave.

Archie grinned. "Best one yet."

Chapter 20

Six Weeks Later

The bell jingled as Archie opened the front door of the dentist's office. Instead of taking the bus home, he'd asked Zig's parents to drop him here. Mom was leaving work early so they could grab dinner, just the two of them.

It had been far too long since they'd played hooky for a few hours. Today, they were sneaking off to try a new burger place between Ithaca and St. Louis. Archie could practically taste the milkshake already.

"Archie!" Zahira called from the front desk. She leaned forward and lowered her voice. "How's that secret project going?"

"Great, actually," Archie whispered. "The firefighters have been helping a ton." When he'd told people at the station about his plan, they'd jumped on it like it was a four-alarm fire. They'd shared all kinds of information with Archie and even offered to put him in touch with other people who could help.

"Sweet! Secret handshake time, go!" Zahira held out her fist, which Archie bumped. When she spoke again, her voice was raised so Penny would hear them. "So, you decide to marry me yet?"

"I keep forgetting to ask Mom if it's okay."

"Oh, she knows I'd make an awesome daughter-in-law. Right, Penny?"

"Run for your life, Archie," Mom called from an examination room.

Zahira shook her head. "That's cold. We don't need her permission, though. Let's elope."

"Cool, I just need to find a ring," Archie said. "And a job so I can afford a ring."

Mom appeared from the examination room, leaving the door open behind her. Archie could see a patient lying on one of those weird chairs. Some kind of dentist's torture gadget was covering his mouth.

"So, the appliance will need to stay in for another twenty minutes, then he's finished," Mom said to Zahira. She raised her voice to say, "Have a good evening, Mr. Turner."

The man in the chair raised two thumbs. "Hoo goo."

"Thanks," Mom said like she understood perfectly. "Good night, Zahira."

"Bye, Penny. Bye, husband, I love you!"

As they headed for the car, Archie said, "I didn't know you spoke Dentist Patient. What'd he say?"

"Oh, yeah, I don't even notice it anymore. He said, *you too*. So, ready for dinner?"

"That burger's not going to eat itself."

~~~

Mom tucked her phone away. "Aunt Violet made it to the house."

"Hope she doesn't try feeding Grandpa one of her tofu steaks again," Archie said.

They weren't so bad, but Grandpa couldn't get used to the texture. Or the fact that they weren't beef.

"Still, it's nice that everyone's helping more," said Mom. "Clara has been a godsend, but your Grandpa still does better around family, I think."

That was one change Archie hadn't liked—or rather, he hadn't liked that they needed it now. The nurse Aunt Candace had hired came to the house five days per week, plus one or two evenings, to help look after Grandpa. Depending on the day, Grandpa himself varied between being happy to have her company and confused about who she was and why she was in his house.

There had been a couple of scary days when he'd been angry that an intruder had walked through the front door. But some buried part of Grandpa could still remember how the real Raymond Reese treated people. He'd always told Archie, "Respect people, even when you're not sure they've earned it, and the good ones will rise to meet it." That attitude seemed to have won out with Clara, who treated Grandpa with unfailing patience and understanding. Lately, even when he wasn't in a welcoming frame of mind, he accepted her presence like she was part of the furniture.

He still had good days when he acted like his old self, when he looked at his photo albums or listened to his favorite music and seemed briefly transformed. But even Archie could see they were happening less often. Now, on the bad days, he needed someone keeping an eye on him at all times, and . . .

Archie pushed away the dark thoughts. This

was supposed to be a break—one he and Mom both needed. He made himself refocus on that.

"Totally," he said, taking a monster bite. His eyes rolled back in his head from flavor overload. "Thith ith the greateth burger ever."

"So," Mom said. "You won't tell us anything? Not even a hint?"

Archie took an extra moment to savor the thick-cut bacon, fried egg, and chipotle cheese sauce. He would definitely have to bring Zig here and get him to recreate it.

"A hint?" He tapped his chin theatrically, as if debating. "Hmm . . ."

It had been six weeks since arm wrestling Spencer, apologizing to Desta, talking honestly with Grandpa, and having his grand epiphany. The subject he'd chosen for the Stone-Katzman Project still felt perfect.

Perfect for Archie, at least. Not everyone would get what he was trying to do. He was determined to follow his own advice to Desta, though, and take a chance. He'd turned in his essay two weeks ago and was now fully focused on the presentation. The others in the group were down to finishing touches, which meant they had plenty of time to help. Desta in particular had jumped in with sunny determination, calling his plan *ambitious*.

Something had shifted between them after his apology. Whenever they saw each other now, she gave him a big smile, and it felt like they could talk forever without running out of things to say. Whether that would make them more than friends, he still wasn't sure, and he still hadn't worked up the nerve to ask. But it was nice.

Mom playfully tossed a fry at him. "Fine, keep your secrets. Turns out I don't *want* to know."

Archie had insisted on keeping the details to himself. Only his study group knew what he was planning, and even they had just the broad strokes. Still, it might be nice to share a little.

"Fine. One hint."

Mom's carefully hidden enthusiasm burst into a wide smile. Archie pulled his project folder from his bag and laid one sheet on the table for Mom to see. The paper displayed a diagram.

"Here's the floor plan for the exhibit hall. Can you guess which project booth is mine?"

Brow furrowed, she studied the diagram. The exhibit hall was divided into four sections, with an open circle in the center to allow for foot traffic.

There were aisles between sections, then smaller aisles within each. From above, it resembled the grid pattern of a city. Instead of buildings, there were project booths, each one its own square.

"Hm," Mom said, eyeing Archie now. "I'm trying to decide if you'd pick a booth near the front just to get it over with, or near the back for dramatic effect."

"Give up?"

"Never."

"Fine, then no hint."

Mom tossed another fry at him. "Spill it!"

"Okay, okay. My booth's not at the front or the back. It's here."

Archie placed the tip of his finger on the center of the sheet, in the circle between the four squares.

"The big space in the middle?" Mom said. "I didn't think they allowed booths there."

"They usually don't, but you know how Blue Sun wants us all to be free spirits. I told Mr. Gertner it would *stifle my artistic expression* if I couldn't use that spot. Not the whole thing, just the center."

"Wow," Mom said, looking impressed. "You must have something big planned."

"Well, it's big to me."

She smiled. "Then I can't wait to see it."

~~~

They took their time at dinner, and it still passed too quickly. Until now, Archie hadn't realized just how tightly wound they had both become this year.

He felt a stab of guilt at enjoying being away from Grandpa—especially now that their relationship had grown so much. Archie was still getting used to seeing Raymond Reese as a human, with flaws and vulnerabilities. As time went on, though, he'd been surprised to realize that truth was more satisfying than fantasy.

He reminded himself it wasn't Grandpa they were taking a break from—it was the disease. Alzheimer's was the enemy, and you couldn't battle an enemy every minute of every day without burning out.

So Archie made himself settle back in the passenger seat and enjoy the ride while Mom navigated toward home. The country backroads were beautiful in the evening light as the sun set behind the trees.

"That's funny," Mom muttered.

Rousing, Archie saw they were almost home. Their driveway was coming up, and he could already see their house and its wide green lawn.

"What?" he said.

"That's Candace's car. I thought just Violet came tonight."

"Hm," Archie said, but didn't give it much thought. Relaxation had settled into his bones.

When Mom parked, Archie heaved himself out of the car and lumbered toward the front door, ready to collapse on the couch and watch something funny.

The front door opened. Aunt Candace stood there, barking at someone over her shoulder.

". . . couldn't have gone too far, unless you somehow managed to—" She broke off at the sight of Mom and Archie, her eyes going wide.

Peering inside, Archie could see that her words had been directed at Aunt Violet—who was crying. She looked terrified.

"Oh," Aunt Candace said. "You're back early."

"Penny, I swear I just turned around for five minutes!" Aunt Violet said.

"Huh?" Mom said.

Uncle Dan appeared from around the side of the house. "He's not in the shed or—Oh. Hey, you two. Don't worry, it'll be fine."

A fist of ice clutched Archie's heart and squeezed. He suddenly found it hard to breathe.

"What will?" Mom said.

Aunt Candace pursed her lips, projecting annoyance. But Archie could see genuine fear behind it. "Violet got distracted, and Dad wandered off," she said. "We can't find him."

Chapter 21

thump—thump
thump—thump
breathless, Archie runs
     searches everywhere, trying to see through the
     dusky shadows
          up the driveway where it meets the road
               deep ditches with tall grass
                    no Grandpa

he keeps running
thump—thump
maybe on the road
he peers down it as far as he can see
                    no Grandpa

he keeps running
thump—thump
the fear grows with every step, pushing out every
other feeling, every other sense
until all he can hear
all he can feel
    is his own
    pounding
    heartbeat

thump—thump
the family runs too, searching, calling out
  Archie sees their mouths move but cannot hear
    no response
     no Grandpa

thump—thump
Archie runs
  his legs burn
  lungs heavy like an elephant sits on his chest
  searches the utility shed
    no Grandpa

thump—thump
the house blazes, all lights on
not in there, Archie knows somehow he just knows
> he turns, house behind him now
>> faces the tree line where backyard ends and
>> forest begins
>>> then the creek

and Archie knows

thump—thump thump—thump thump—thump
scrambles forward through brush and branches and
thorns pushing through
keep going keep searching Grandpa always loved
these woods was never afraid
they belonged to him he was never

there
just visible
> a wrinkled hand

everything blurs
Archie is there in an instant, collapsing to his knees
his chest rumbles, his throat catches fire
    he cannot hear it, but he knows
        he is screaming

        Grandpa will not wake up
            blood ohgodtheresblood
thumpthumpthumpthumpthumpthumpthumpthump
thumpthumpthumpthumpthumpthump

focus deep breath focus think
he grabs Grandpa's wrist
taught how to check in health class
    never thought he would use it
    wait for it
    it will be there it will be there it will
        Thump—thump
        Thump—thump
        Thump—thump
           Archie's eyes burn with relieved tears
           Still alive

Footsteps approach he can feel them.

Gentle hands are moving him aside. His family is there. They speak but the words are muffled. Grandpa must have stumbled, fallen, bumped his head.

Lights flash in the distance. Someone called and they're coming to help . . .

~~~

The ambulance swerved into their driveway. Archie took what felt like his first full breath in hours.

The first sound he heard was the siren.

Chapter 22

It was storming again.

Two days after Grandpa's fall and his trip to the emergency room, the family sat around the dining room table, discussing what should happen next. Once again, Archie felt like he was stuck in those gray clouds. None of this felt real.

"I can try to be here more," Aunt Violet said. She wore dark colors today and was more somber than Archie had ever seen her. "Work might let me rearrange my schedule, and I can skip being in any plays next season."

"I can try to hire more nurses," Mom said. "Set up some kind of rotating schedule."

"Just send us the bill," Dan said. "Whatever it is, we'll cover it."

"Penny," Aunt Candace said, her expression

pained, "that may not be enough. If he wanders off again and gets *really* hurt, they could slap you with a liability—"

"Can you not be a lawyer, just this once?" Mom said.

"I'm only trying to help."

"Then do you have a solution?"

"Well, I know that we—"

"Guys, please, we all love each other, we're just—"

"All I'm saying is—"

Everything blurred together. Words and emotions buffeted Archie as they gusted back and forth across the table. He sat silent, unsure whether he wanted to shout or cry or stuff himself with junk food until he couldn't feel anything.

Directly across from him, Grandpa sat with hands folded on the table. He wore a bandage on his head where he'd knocked it against a tree branch. The wound wasn't too deep, so the bandage would come off soon. The mild concussion had been far scarier, but Grandpa seemed to have recovered.

He stared into space, looking calm. He didn't say much, but Archie knew he was listening to every word. Ironically, he'd been lucid since the accident. So why wasn't he saying anything?

As if he'd heard Archie's question, Grandpa locked eyes with him. They stared at each other across the table, sharing a quiet moment, a look that said how awful it was that this had come and life could totally stink sometimes but hey that was life. Right?

Then Grandpa's eyes turned sad—the saying-goodbye kind of sad. He stood up, drew a folded pamphlet out of his pocket, and set it on the table.

"This is what we're doing," he said in a tone that brooked no more debate.

Mom grabbed the pamphlet. "Dad, where did you get this? *When* did you get this?"

"I put it in motion months ago, when I still had my whole mind," Grandpa said. "You're all dancing around this, but none of you wants to say it. Well, *I'm* saying it. I'm making this decision for myself. So let's talk about the next step."

Archie stared at the pamphlet as if it were a poisonous snake. Every cell in his body screamed in protest.

A retirement home. A really nice one with people specifically trained to handle Alzheimer's patients, but still a retirement home. The kind of place where—according to every movie that featured one—people went to die.

If Grandpa went there, it would mean that he didn't live with them anymore. That he probably never would again.

The discussion lasted another hour. The adults protested in their own ways, trying to find different solutions. Grandpa batted away each objection and alternative calmly yet resolutely. As if he knew they needed to wear themselves out before accepting that he was right and this was really going to happen.

Archie had no words to offer. Earth had tilted off its axis and gravity had turned sideways, and all he could do was fall. He sat there, feeling smaller than ever.

Eventually, everyone quieted. When Grandpa spoke again, his words were gentle but strong as steel.

"I'm a grown man with my own money—and, for now, my own mind. I'm making my own decision while I still can," he said. "I'm doing this for me, 'cause I can relax if I know there's someone watching, ready to keep me from hurting anybody, including myself. And I'm doing this for you. You're my family and I love you. This is my last chance to take care of *you*. So, for God's sake, let me do it."

Archie knew that was that. It was decided. The world he'd known his entire life was over.

~~~

It was late and everyone had gone home. Archie sagged in his desk chair, staring at nothing, his fingers absently rifling through the pages Aunt Violet had printed out for them. She'd been researching local support groups for families of Alzheimer's patients.

There were some promising options. Other people who were losing loved ones to the same disease, sharing resources and tips and understanding.

The family was going to need that in the coming weeks. Months.

Years.

It was a wonderful gesture. Archie knew that, at some point, he would be able to feel grateful that Aunt Violet was looking out for her family's emotional health. That was very much like her.

Right now, though, Archie only felt like someone had pulled a plug from his body and drained him until he was empty.

He should have said something. Even clumsy words would have expressed how he felt about this. Grandpa would have heard them and he would have—

"Hey, Fletch."

Archie spun his chair around. Grandpa stood in the doorway, wearing a face that looked as drawn and tired as Archie felt. "How ya feeling?"

Archie had no time to fight it. In an instant, everything bubbled up inside him like a volcano and spilled over. "You're supposed to be here," he said, hot tears pouring down his cheeks. "You're supposed to be here for all of it."

Grandpa crossed the room and pulled Archie into a strong embrace. He understood, as Archie had known he would.

The many events that would be coming in Archie's and Mom's lives. Archie growing up, graduating, that first job, that first time falling in love. Getting married, even Mom getting married again maybe. Having kids of his own. Adventures and stories big and small would be around every corner, and Archie had always assumed Grandpa would be there for them.

Grandpa held on while Archie cried and raged and cried again, as if his tears could beat back the tide of what life had thrown at them. He lost track of how long it lasted. When he finally began to feel calm, Grandpa loosened his grip enough to lean back and look Archie in the eyes.

"I'm so grateful for the time we've had these last

few months," he said. "Our talks. Those stories you created for us. It's meant so much to me."

Archie blinked. The stories, the fantasies. Maybe they hadn't been useless. Or at least, they hadn't been meaningless. They'd given him and Grandpa a chance to spend time together, to feel close even as the disease tried to drive them apart. He hadn't considered that before.

"Life's an adventure, Fletch," he said. "You've got so many to come. I've got one left. A last leap into the unknown. You know what? I'm okay with it. I want you to be okay with it too."

Archie shook his head in silent protest.

"And if some god shall wreck me in the wine-dark sea, even so I will endure," Grandpa said. "For already have I suffered, and much have I toiled in perils of waves and war. So let this new disaster come. It only makes one more."

Seeing Archie's look of confusion, he offered a wistful smile.

"That's from *The Odyssey*. It means I'm tired and I'm hurting, but I'm ready for what's to come." Reaching up, he swiped the tears from Archie's face. "This is just life, Fletch. It happens. We'll face whatever comes, and in the end . . . we'll be okay."

Chapter 23

Archie stood at the entrance to the exhibit hall. He wore his best suit—well, his only suit—with a shiny new tie that Uncle Dan had given him to mark the occasion.

He patted the left side of his jacket for the hundredth time. His essay was nestled in the inside pocket, waiting to be revealed. Actually, he should stop calling it an essay now and start calling it a speech. The top five had been announced a few days ago, and Archie and Desta were on the list. For an aspiring writer, that had been a proud moment.

Inside, he was a strange mix of emotions. Happy that this night was finally here. Proud of what he'd created, yet nervous about how it would be received. Hopeful that people would like it—especially certain people.

Especially one person.

He wanted tonight to feel special. Tomorrow, Grandpa would move into his retirement home. Once the decision had been made, it had come together too quickly. Archie practically had whiplash from how fast everything was changing.

By the end of tomorrow, it would all be different. But that was tomorrow.

His family approached, dressed like they were going to the opera. The academy treated the Stone-Katzman Project like an important occasion, so everyone wore their best. Aunt Candace and Uncle Dan were in the lead, followed by Aunt Violet, then Mom with her arm looped through Grandpa's.

Archie tried to catch Grandpa's eye, but his gaze was clouded over. He glanced back and forth, studying his surroundings without recognizing anything. Archie's heart sank. He had hoped the real Raymond Reese would be here tonight, but what Archie read about "sundowning" had turned out to be true: Alzheimer's patients often grew less alert and more confused in the evening.

Another fantasy that hadn't come true.

"Wow," Uncle Dan said, shaking Archie's hand.

"They didn't tell us James Bond would be here. Nice suit."

Archie laughed. "You all look great too."

"So where's this secret project?" Aunt Candace said.

"I'm literally dying to see it," Aunt Violet added.

"Follow me."

As he led them into the exhibit hall, a wave of festive sound washed over them. The cavernous hall was packed with students, family, and academy alumni. The crowds roamed up and down the grid-patterned rows, enjoying the results of nearly a year's work from all the eighth graders. Even Archie had been astounded by some of the results.

"This way," he said over his shoulder and plunged into the crowd.

They passed Kamiko's quadruple-sized booth, which she had turned into a pen filled with dogs and cats and some less common animals in need of rescue. Actually, the word *pen* didn't fully capture what Kamiko had accomplished. She had turned a corner of the exhibit hall into a full-on animal sanctuary, with a squad of volunteers from the shelter caring for the animals and running the adoption program. Kamiko presided over it all like a pro, looking happier than

Archie had ever seen her. From the crowd around her booth, he guessed she wouldn't have a single animal left to rescue by the end of the night.

Spencer's booth was nearby. Archie had been able to see it up close before the exhibit hall opened, yet he felt astonished all over again as he walked by. True to his word, Spencer had completely abandoned his first idea. His new plan was to go to law school, then work pro bono—representing people in desperate need who couldn't afford to pay for legal help.

His booth was surprisingly understated. It displayed his top choices of law schools and professional specialties, along with notes on how he'd use his law degree to help protect the little guy from big corporations. Spencer had forgone his usual muscle shirt for a tailored gray suit, and in place of a cocky grin there was an earnest expression as he spoke about the human right to clean drinking water.

They were getting close. Eagerness, intertwined with fear, writhed around in Archie's stomach. He suppressed the anxiety as much as he could.

Passing Zig's booth helped. Archie smelled it from fifty feet away, and as they drew close he saw Zig using his wok to sear the scallops for his ramen dish. The crowd *ooohe*d.

They reached the open space at the center of the exhibit hall. Traffic flowed along the outer edge of the circle, scores of people passing from one area to the next.

His family stopped in their tracks. He watched their faces, savoring the open jaws, the gasps, the way Mom covered her mouth in surprise.

Archie didn't have a regular booth, or really a booth at all. Instead he had placed a large glass display case on the floor, with five temporary walls extending out from the case like the rays of a star.

Desta had found the case in the art studio's storage room, and a few of Grandpa's firefighter friends had supplied the walls. Desta had helped Archie design the setup to mimic the feel of an art gallery, so people could move easily from one wall to the next, always keeping that central display in view. Then the whole project group—along with a few firefighters—had helped Archie erect it in the exhibit hall.

Speaking of firefighters, four of them were here. All of them had been trained by Raymond Reese. They stood near Archie's display, ready to share stories about the man who had taught them so much about protecting their fellow humans. Archie's heart burst with joy as they welcomed Grandpa.

Archie had made sure the display was well lit, and he'd set wireless speakers at each corner to play Grandpa's favorite songs.

A large three-sided sign sat on top of the case, announcing the title of his project. It read WHAT I WANT TO BE. Except WHAT was crossed out, and written above it was WHO.

Inside the glass case, Archie had arranged years' worth of relics from Grandpa's days as a firefighter. The dress uniform, the rescue gear, the Medal of Valor he had been awarded for risking his life. On each wall, a different quote was written in large block letters. Archie watched his family as they read the quotes and thrilled at the recognition in their eyes. Each one was from Grandpa—his wisdom about what mattered in life.

Around each quote, Archie had arranged old photos showing Grandpa in all the stages of his life, newspaper clippings of things he'd accomplished in service to others, and even written stories that Archie had convinced more of Grandpa's old friends and colleagues to send him. Stories about Raymond Reese—the man he was and the way he had lived. How people had trusted and admired and relied on him. How he had made mistakes and learned from them, grown from them, used them as fuel to do better. Archie watched his family absorb it all, working to hold back his own tears as theirs traced down their faces.

When they had questions, Archie answered. Mostly, though, he stood back and let the project speak for itself, swelling with pride as they reacted to each element. All the while, he hoped they could take enough pictures and video to share with Grandpa, so that on a good day he could enjoy it.

"I love this song," Grandpa said, leaning on Mom's arm. "Your Grandma Ella and I used to dance to it."

Something had shifted. Grandpa's eyes were clear and sharp. When he looked at Archie, he was really seeing him. When he looked at the display walls, he read the words and saw the photos and reacted just like himself. "You outdid yourself, Fletch. I feel like I just woke up. I just wish your grandma could be here to see this. She'd be so proud of you."

Archie couldn't speak. Grandpa patted his shoulder with a knowing expression.

"Let's just enjoy it, okay? Don't know how long I've got, and I don't want to miss a minute."

Archie nodded, overcome with gratitude. Whatever happened tomorrow, at least they would always have this.

"Have to admit, though," Grandpa said. He hesitated, taking in Archie's work with a sweeping glance. "I'm not sure I've earned all this. I'm just an ordinary man, Archie."

"I know you are," Archie assured him. "You're an ordinary man, *and* you're my hero, flaws and all. You always will be."

This time Grandpa was speechless. Archie gave his back a reassuring pat. As he did, he glanced over Grandpa's shoulder and saw that the crown jewel of his project had just arrived. The woman was about thirty, and she looked both anxious and excited.

Grandpa seemed lost in thought, so Archie left him with Mom and stepped away to greet the newcomer.

"Thank you so much for coming," he said as they shook hands.

"Thank *you* for finding me," she said. "I'm so happy to be here."

"Aunt Candace, Uncle Dan, Aunt Violet," Archie said, then gestured to the woman. "Meet Isabelle."

"It's such a pleasure," Isabelle said, shaking each of their hands.

"Um, likewise," Uncle Dan said.

"Who are you again?" Aunt Candace said.

Archie glanced over his shoulder. Grandpa was

still absorbed in looking at the display. He hadn't turned around yet. Still, Archie nodded to Isabelle, encouraging her to go ahead with her story.

"Twenty years ago, I almost died in a fire," Isabelle said. "My mother and I were trapped in our apartment. I remember her crying. At nine years old, I knew I was going to die there."

Grandpa had half-turned toward Isabelle now.

"But then the smoke parted, and a man was there," Isabelle said. "We could barely move, so he picked us up and ran. Fire and smoke didn't stop him. Burning things fell on him and he just kept going. And then we were safe."

Recognition shone from Aunt Candace's face. Her eyes glittered with tears. "He used to tell us about that fire," she said. "He told us about you and your mother."

"What are you doing now?" Archie prompted.

"I'm a pediatrician," Isabelle said. "I try to help kids too. For twenty years I've wanted to find that firefighter. I . . ."

Isabelle cut off as Grandpa finally turned around and stepped toward her. For an eternal moment they stared. Then they reached for each other and collapsed into an embrace.

Archie watched their reunion with pure joy, no longer caring about whatever else happened tonight. He wiped away happy tears as Grandpa met, for the second time, the little girl whose life he had saved. Whatever anyone thought about how strange his project might be, none of that mattered. Because it had accomplished exactly what Archie hoped.

For Raymond Reese to know the legacy he was leaving behind, to understand that others would carry forward what he had started.

And that he would be remembered.

Chapter 24

"You're a hit," Zig said.

Archie stood inside Zig's booth, wolfing down a bowl of the best ramen he'd ever tasted. "I think you have me confused with my best friend. You're the one who's a hit."

He nodded to the line that started from Zig's booth and looped around the corner. Some people were there for a second or third time. Archie had no doubt that one day his friend would rock the culinary world.

Zig had gone beyond just making ramen. He'd also created awesome little dessert spheres. The outside was pleasantly chewy and vanilla, while the gooey middle tasted like green tea. People had actually applauded those. Everyone loved Zig.

"I'm just glad they like it." Zig shrugged modestly. "I've heard people talking about yours. They've never seen one like it. And I saw your family's faces—they were really proud."

As Archie savored another bite, he stole a glance at his own display. There did seem to be constant traffic through it, and people were taking their time with every wall. Isabelle and the firefighters stood by the glass case, eager to share their stories.

His family had offered plenty of praise and Archie had tried his best to absorb every word. What he would remember most, though, was the look in Grandpa's eyes. They both knew this moment was special.

"I should get back," Archie said, slurping down the last of his noodles. "Awesome job, Zig."

"Thanks, bro. Have fun."

Archie took his time meandering through the crowd. A little more relaxed now, he could soak up the atmosphere inside the exhibit hall. He could fully appreciate the effort everyone else had put into their projects.

His wasn't the only one with surprises. One girl had replaced her booth with a huge plexiglass tank, filled it with salt water and various forms of marine life, then donned a mermaid costume and spent the evening swimming. Archie had no idea what that meant for her future, but it sure was unexpected.

Though not half as unexpected as what he saw now. Spencer Harrington stood at one of Archie's walls—the *A Few Brave Moments Can Change Your Whole Life* display—examining the photos of Grandpa's travels around the world, the unusual jobs he'd done to fund them, and the people he'd met along the way.

They still weren't exactly friends, but there had been a sort of unspoken truce ever since the arm-wrestling match. Still, old habit made Archie put up his guard. Approaching the wall, he stood quietly next to Spencer.

They stood side by side and studied the wall, not facing each other. Archie waited.

Eventually Spencer squared his shoulders. "Yours is the best one."

Archie's eyebrows climbed. It must have felt like lifting a truck for Spencer to admit that.

"Thanks."

Grandpa's voice replayed in his head. *Respect people, even when you're not sure they've earned it, and the good ones will rise to meet it.*

"You're really serious about your project?" Archie asked.

Spencer nodded.

"My aunt's a lawyer. Not the same kind as you want to be, but if I asked, I'll bet she would be happy to help. You know, point you in the right direction or something."

Spencer blinked, as if seeing Archie anew. "Thanks." He hesitated. "I'm gonna train hard this summer. Try to get in better shape for freshman teams next year."

"*Better* shape?" Archie said, incredulous.

Spencer laughed. "Anyway, got a killer gym at my house, and some of the guys are coming to train with me. We . . . could use another strong guy."

"Really?"

"You spot me on bench press, I'll teach you how to run." Spencer affected a shrug. "You know, if you want to."

Archie couldn't believe that he was about to say this—or that he actually meant it. "Um, yeah, okay. Sounds good."

"Good." Spencer gave a curt nod. "Well. Uh, see you later then."

Spencer headed for his own booth, leaving Archie in a cloud of *did-that-really-just-happen*. He had no idea if the two of them could ever be actual friends. But he would settle for mutual respect.

Archie felt genuinely good in a way that he hadn't in a long time. As he savored the feeling, the crowds parted enough for him to see another row of project booths. Just enough to get his first glimpse of her.

Desta's smile was visible even from here. As she moved, her black dress sparkled subtly in the bright lights.

Then Archie noticed details about her booth. It was too far away to tell for sure, but he thought he saw . . . no way. Had she really changed her whole display without telling anyone?

Slipping through the crowd, he approached her booth and drank in every wonderful, surprising detail.

"Hey, Desta."

"Archie!"

Her smile got bigger. He hadn't realized that was possible. Leaning across the table, she pulled him into a hug. Archie let himself enjoy it as her scent wafted over him. The hug was over too quickly.

"I love your booth," she said. "Really. It's like my favorite ever. Don't tell Kam I said that."

"Thanks." Archie glanced around her booth with a significant smile. "Same to you."

Desta turned bashful, tucking a lock of hair

behind her ear. "Last-minute change. I decided on it literally the night before our essays were due. And then I figured I'd just let the presentation be a surprise, like yours. My parents still aren't convinced, but . . . well, I had to do what felt right."

"Your art is amazing!" a seventh-grade girl exclaimed as she bounded up to Desta's booth. "You really drew all these?"

"Everything on this side," Desta said, gesturing to her right. "The other side is the artists I'm learning from."

There were pieces here that Archie hadn't seen before. Desta had been brave enough to show works in progress. The booth walls were also covered in white paper, and she had drawn designs that flowed between her work and the other artists'. Somehow it created the illusion that every drawing was part of one large piece.

Her talent really was staggering. Whatever happened in the future, Archie was glad she was letting herself embrace it tonight.

He also couldn't help marveling at how gracious she was with people who stopped to compliment her work. It hadn't seemed possible, but Archie's admiration for Desta Senai grew even more.

As the seventh grader moved on, Desta bent to straighten a few drawings laid out on the table. She handled every piece as if it was precious.

There was a break in the traffic now, when no one else was approaching. A quiet moment.

His moment.

Self-doubt roared to life, chasing away the confidence he'd built up. He couldn't do this!

Slow down. Breathe.

Archie took a deep breath. He turned toward his own display in the center of the hall, catching a glimpse of his favorite wall. He read the words for a thousandth time.

A Few Brave Moments Can Change Your Whole Life.

His heart pounded. That was okay, he told himself. It was okay to be afraid. You couldn't be brave if you weren't afraid first.

"You look beautiful tonight," he said.

Desta turned to him, her eyes going wide. Archie wasn't sure if that was a good or bad kind of shock, but there was only one way to find out for sure.

"You always do," he continued. "But tonight I have the guts to say it."

Desta stared. "Um, th-thank you."

"Grandpa and I talked a lot, this year, about how

to be the right kind of man. He says a big part of it is honesty. Life is short, so you can't be afraid to say how you feel. You know?"

Desta nodded, still looking stunned. Archie glanced down, taking a moment to gather himself. Then he stood straight, shoulders back, and met her gaze.

"I really like you. You treat people like they matter, you're not afraid to show you care about things, and you're fun to be around." He paused to settle his nerves again but found that he didn't need to. This felt right. "I don't know if you think of me like that. If not, it's okay. But if you do feel like we could be something more than friends, it'd be great if you wanted to call me sometime."

He paused so she could respond if she wanted. For once, though, Desta was the one at a loss for words. She looked at him as if seeing him for the first time.

"Personally," he added, "I think we'd be great together."

"Um, I . . ."

It seemed to be all she could manage. That was okay. It would all be okay.

Archie smiled. "Good night, Desta."

Turning, he melted into the crowd. He heard her stammer one more time but resisted the urge to go back. He would give her space so she could decide what she wanted.

Whatever happened now, he had taken the leap.

Chapter 25

"Art may not save the world. Not directly," Desta said. "But it can make the world a place worth saving. A home that we fill with beauty and magic and possibility. A canvas where we add our own brushstrokes, then pass it on to the next generation so they can add theirs. Because where there's art, there's hope. And I think that can save lives too."

With a satisfied nod, Desta stepped back from the podium. The crowd applauded. Her friends shouted her name as she stepped down from the stage.

It was a full house. Everyone had left the exhibit hall and packed into the auditorium to hear the five speeches. Desta had gone first, and she had set a high bar.

Mrs. Kirkpatrick, Blue Sun Academy's principal, reappeared onstage to introduce the next student.

Archie didn't register a word of what she said. The other speeches flowed past him like a river of muted sound punctuated by the thumping of his own heart. He'd never spoken in front of this many people before.

Finally, Mrs. Kirkpatrick called Archie's name. As he approached the stage, he caught words from the principal like *unorthodox* and *thought-provoking*. Was that good?

He shook off the self-doubt. It didn't matter. He had already taken the leap, and now he was determined to enjoy the flight. Stepping up to the podium, Archie unfolded his notes and gazed out at the crowd.

"They say you should never meet your heroes. It'll always be disappointing," he began. "But they never met mine. I lived with my hero for thirteen years. I heard his words, saw his choices, and I was never disappointed, even in the most . . . human moments. My biggest hope wasn't that he'd live up to my expectations, but that I'd live up to his. That I'd make him proud."

Archie glanced instinctively toward Grandpa. In the split second that their eyes met, he saw exactly that. Pride. He suppressed a wave of emotion before continuing.

"The future is scary when you're thirteen. We wake up every day facing a fog. We charge into the unknown and try to find our way. Some days we get lost and all we can do is sit while the fog rolls over us. But on the good days, we remember our heroes. We borrow the light they used to find their way—light made of truth and just a little bit of fantasy—and we use it to find our own way. We try, and if we fail, we try again and do our best to get it right. Hopefully we make that light brighter, so that one day we can lend it to someone else who needs it. When that day comes, I hope I remember where my light came from. I hope I can look back and see my hero, Raymond Reese—father, teacher, and protector. I hope I'll see that I made him proud. If I can do that, then it'll mean I did something right."

Archie let his gaze sweep over the audience, wanting to meet as many eyes as he could.

"The Stone-Katzman Project is supposed to be about the future. Some people think that means a career. We start high school next year, so adults say it's time for us to figure out what we're going to do with our lives. Well, I still have no clue what I'm going to do—not five years from now, or ten, or twenty. But I have learned who I want to be. Something tells me that's what matters most."

He gripped the podium. Almost there.

"So, thank you for this. Whatever you do, however you find your way through the fog, I hope you remember what makes it worthwhile. The people who travel through the fog with you, the lessons they teach you, and the purpose you find that gives your life meaning. I hope your life's work isn't just a job, but becoming the person you want to be. And when you get there . . . I hope you're happy."

Archie stepped back from the podium and walked away. Halfway across the stage, he realized the room was pin-drop silent. The only thing he heard was his own footsteps.

He felt a flash of panic. Was the speech that bad?

As his feet hit the stairs, the auditorium exploded in thunderous applause. Archie's heart leapt as the wave of sound crashed over him, nearly pushing him back physically.

Everyone was on their feet. Stunned, Archie searched for faces he knew. Grandpa was clasping his hands and pumping them in the air with a victorious cheer. Mom was crying the good kind of tears.

He'd taken the leap and somehow landed on his feet.

"Time for a classie!" Zig called.

Then Archie was surrounded by his classmates. They pressed together, smiling and striking poses while Zig snapped pictures.

Archie knew he would never forget this.

This was one of the moments Grandpa talked about.

Chapter 26

They finished far too quickly.

First thing in the morning, the family had come together to help Grandpa move into his new home. By early afternoon they had unloaded and arranged everything he wanted to bring to the assisted living complex. Except one last box—a small one that Grandpa wanted to carry in himself.

They stood in the front courtyard of the complex now, cooling off after the move, enjoying the sunshine and the spring breeze as it whispered through the trees. A few paces away, Archie watched as Grandpa interacted with the rest of the family. He was having a good day.

None of that seemed fair. A day like today should be gloomy and gray, and Grandpa shouldn't seem so normal. This way, with everything bright and everyone well, didn't match the underlying truth that had made this happen in the first place.

Archie did his best to be cheerful. His family obviously needed it.

It seemed like Archie only blinked, and the time had arrived. Grandpa set down his little box and said goodbye to his daughters. Starting with Mom, then Aunt Candace and Aunt Violet, he hugged them tightly, paused to speak softly with each of them and to wipe away their tears.

He shook hands with Uncle Dan. Then they pulled each other into a fierce hug, exchanging words too quiet for Archie to hear. The two men had always been good friends, and it was plain to see the friendship would continue as long as it could. When they parted, Uncle Dan's eyes were red, and he and Aunt Candace clung to each other.

Then Grandpa was there in front of him. Archie managed to maintain his brave face.

"Can Fletch and I get a moment to ourselves?" Grandpa asked.

The others agreed and turned to head to their cars. There was a quiet moment while Archie and Grandpa waited for them to climb inside and shut the doors. Then it was just the two of them.

"I left something for you back at home," Grandpa said. "The Ireland painting. I know you like it. Maybe you can paint your own someday, after you see it for yourself."

"Deal," Archie said. "And thanks."

He tried but couldn't think of anything meaningful to say. So he reached for the first thing that occurred to him. "I told Desta everything last night."

Grandpa beamed. "That's never easy. Good for you!"

Archie shrugged. "Well, she hasn't answered yet."

"It doesn't matter. You took the leap, and that's what counts. You're a brave man. Which reminds me."

Bending down, Grandpa reached into the last box and pulled out a book bound in worn brown leather—the Journal. Except it looked different. Archie studied it, momentarily puzzled, before realizing all the stickers were gone.

"This is yours now," Grandpa said. "I think you're ready for the whole story. Oh, and there's one more thing."

Grandpa dug into the box once more, and came back with another leather-bound book. This one was thinner, the binding newer. He handed that over too.

"Here's something no one else knows," Grandpa

said. "Over this past year, when I could remember things and felt up to it, I wrote more stories. Some are old memories, some are recent. And some tell about my adventures with a very special young man—one who cared so much about me that, at times when I felt the most lost, I remembered who I was."

Archie nearly lost his brave face. A heavy lump rose in his throat. He could feel his eyes getting glassy, and Grandpa's were doing the same.

This isn't goodbye, he promised himself. *I'll see him again tomorrow, and next week.*

The thought kept him from going to pieces. This wasn't the end—not even close. Still, it was *an* end, and right now they both felt it more than ever.

Grandpa swallowed hard. When he spoke, his voice trembled. "Remember me, Archie," he said. "If I know someone does, then . . . well, maybe this last adventure won't be half bad."

"We'll all remember," Archie said. "I'll make sure of it. I promise."

Grandpa nodded and gulped down a deep breath. It occurred to Archie then—he was the only one Grandpa had let see him this way. Sad, afraid, but still determined.

"I'll . . . I'll see you soon, okay, Fletch?"

"Real soon," Archie said.

With a nod, Grandpa picked up his box and walked toward the building's front entrance. To Archie it seemed like a mile-long march. He was determined to stay there and watch until his grandfather got safely inside.

Seized by curiosity, Archie flipped open the front cover of the new Journal. To his surprise, there was a letter addressed to him on the first page.

Fletch,

I've never told anyone why I started calling you that. I'm telling you now. Back in the old days, fletchers made the arrows for an archer. I called you Fletch because, in my own unusual way, it reminded me to help you make yourself into something special. To help you become the right kind of person, and then aim yourself at what really matters in life. I don't really know how much I helped, but I do see the person you're becoming. I'm already proud of him.

In Love and Adventure Always,
Raymond Reese
Grandpa

By the time Archie finished reading, the tears were falling. He didn't try to stop them. Closing the new Journal, he looked up.

Grandpa stood just in front of the entrance, peering back at Archie. The box sat at his feet. With a broad smile, he lifted his arms and affected the motion of pulling back an arrow, then releasing it into the sky.

Laughing through his tears, Archie did the same. Then Grandpa picked up his box, gave one last wave, and stepped inside. The door closed behind him.

Archie gazed down at both Journals, marveling at what Grandpa had given them all. Whatever happened in the future, Raymond Reese would always be Raymond Reese. Even if his memories disappeared altogether, some would live on in these pages. Even more would live on in the hearts of the people who loved him.

Archie's phone buzzed in his pocket. Taking it out, he saw a text on his screen and his breath caught in his throat.

—*Good time to call?*

A thrill raced through him, followed by a flash of fear. He pushed the fear away and sent a text in response.

—*Sure.*

A moment later his phone buzzed with a call. Archie let it ring twice and then answered.

"Hey, Desta . . . Tonight? That'd be great. I'll have to make sure with Mom, but . . . Oh, thanks. We just moved him in today, actually. Yeah . . ."

Archie paused. Looking back at the doors to the retirement home, he smiled and stood a little taller.

"Yeah. We'll be okay."

Author's Note

I never thought I'd write a book like this.

Anyone who's read my other books will tell you that I love writing character dynamics and dialogue, but I also love epic action scenes and explosions in the sky and small heroes facing huge, universe-ending odds. So, when my mother suggested that I write a story about Alzheimer's, my first response was an immediate and emphatic *no, thank you*. How would that even work? There was no enemy to confront, no mystery to solve, no shocking twist ending.

And how would a book like that be anything but depressing?

In December 2017, Alzheimer's took my grandfather. He, and my family by extension, had been struggling with it for a few years. It's why my mother had suggested the story in the first place. I'd had a front-row seat to what life with an Alzheimer's sufferer was like, both for the afflicted and the family, so I knew I could bring real-life experience to the story. Every family's experience is different, so I couldn't represent every situation, but I could at least represent one. Ours. Still, I resisted.

As my family gathered for his funeral, I listened to their stories, and I saw all those long days written on their faces. The early days, when my mother and her sisters began to think that something was wrong. The later days, when my grandfather would walk into a room full of family with the look in his eye that said he didn't recognize any of us. The thousand days in between, some marked by tears, others by the choice to laugh instead of collapsing under the weight of slow, inevitable sorrow. I heard a hundred more stories from times when I wasn't there, told in tones of remembered desperation, when my grandfather's loved ones would have done anything to bring back the person he had been, if only for a day.

That's when it happened. After I had resisted for more than a year, two ideas occurred to me that changed everything.

The first was a question that became the heart of the story. *How could a boy hold on to hope while his hero was falling to an unstoppable disease?* The second was a version of the very first line of the book. "Grandpa didn't remember me today." From that day on, I saw the characters of Archie and Raymond Reese clearly, and I knew that I had to write their story.

Thanks for sharing it with them.

Acknowledgments

Authors are a quirky bunch. We live in our heads, creating worlds and characters and watching eagerly to see what they'll do next. And because our heads are in the clouds, we surround ourselves with people who walk on solid ground. People we trust to help make our stories the best they can be. Because no author is an island, and no story makes it from idea to printed page without help. A lot of it.

Thanks, Mom, for gently persisting in your assertion that I should write a book about Alzheimer's. You are the reason that you're holding this book in your hands right now. To the rest of my family, thanks for being okay with me writing about this, for borrowing some of your experiences so I could make Archie's story feel as real as possible, and for your support and validation.

To Tricia Skinner, my favorite Sith Lord and galactically awesome agent—thank you for being a tireless advocate for Archie, for all your wise counsel, and for helping me stay focused when I want to juggle a hundred new ideas per week. Thanks also to the whole crew at Fuse Literary, who got behind this book and helped me feel supported. It's so much easier to be creative while having a team I trust at my back.

Which brings me to Amy Fitzgerald, who from day one helped me find ways to make this story deeper and more meaningful. Thanks for your trust, for understanding what I was trying to accomplish, and for being such a great partner to work with. Special thanks to cover artist Chiara Fedele and to everyone on the Lerner team who helped this book make its way into the world, including designer Viet Chu, creative director Danielle Carnito, and production designer Erica Johnson.

Thanks to Amy K. Nichols and the Arizona MG/YA author group. Floating among the clouds is so much better when we have awesome writers to float with us. I treasure the phone calls, the Zoom sessions, hours talking about books and writing craft and the daily life of being an author.

Thanks finally to you, the reader holding this book right now, for riding the dragon along with Archie. I hope it's a story you'll remember.

Questions for Discussion

1. How does Archie's idea of what it means to be a good person change over the course of the story?

2. How does Grandpa's Alzheimer's affect him, Archie, and Mom on a practical level? What about on an emotional level?

3. Even though Archie's fantasies don't stop the progression of Grandpa's Alzheimer's, how do they help both Grandpa and Archie?

4. What does Archie learn about Grandpa's mistakes and regrets, and why is Grandpa still his hero?

5. How do Archie's family and friends help him deal with Grandpa's decline?

6. If you had to do the Stone-Katzman Project, what would your presentation say about your goals for the future?

About the Author

Ryan Dalton spends his time thinking up stories when he's not wearing a cape and fighting crime. He's a singer, a voiceover artist, a pretty decent amateur chef, and a lover of all things geek. Ryan lives in an invisible spaceship that's currently hovering over St. Louis, Missouri. He is also the author of the Time Shift Trilogy.